PRAISE FOR CB SAMET

FOUR-TIME
AWARD-WINNING AUTHOR

"CB Samet is a master of the craft"

— READERS' FAVORITE REVIEW 2017

"CB Samet has a way of bringing you into the hair-raising suspense, keeping you at the edge of your seat"

— VORACIOUS READERS REVIEWER

PRAISE FOR RIVERA FILE

"This is one of my favorite tropes and a romantic thriller of the highest caliber. Don't miss it!"

— GIGI'S READS

"This story is outstanding. It's suspenseful and action packed and definitely entertaining."

— BOOKBUB REVIEWER

"I love this series, and [Rivera File] *is just as good as expected. Full of action, drama, danger, and a love story mixed in with all the adrenaline."*

— GOODREADS REVIEWER

RIVERA FILE

THE RIDER FILES BOOK 9

CB SAMET

AVANTSTAR PUBLISHING

FREE EBOOK WITH NEWSLETTER SIGNUP

In the bustling streets of a sprawling Atlanta metropolis, where shadows dance and danger lurks around every corner, an unlikely love story unfolds amidst the web of a gripping romantic suspense thriller.

When the notorious Chinese mafia sets its sights on tightening its grip over the city's underworld, chaos ensues. As the danger escalates, a resilient female cop, Diz Ocana, finds herself thrust into the heart of her friend's kidnapping.

Meanwhile, skilled and compassionate paramedic Rico Cabrera, has dedicated his life to saving others. Growing up in the same neighborhood as

Diz, he knows firsthand the darkness that plagues their city. Fate reunites them, kindling a connection that defies the boundaries of their respective roles.

*~~~***<<<SIGN UP HERE>>>***~~~*

PROLOGUE

Only the faint spill of moonlight through the windows revealed the pale paintings and tapestries on the walls as Daniela walked through the hallway. The urge to check on Oscar had her tiptoeing in her bare feet with nothing on but her nightgown.

She liked this home—her father's house on the California coast in La Jolla—better than the one on the outskirts of Santiago de Cali in eastern Colombia. California felt safer somehow, which made no logical sense because her father was revered and feared in Colombia while viewed as a criminal in the United States.

Reaching the end of the hall, she pushed open the door to Oscar's room and peeked in on her two-year-old son. He was sleeping soundly, as he did every night. She was both relieved and envious of how well he slept.

What a wondrous delight he'd been these last two years. She was grateful to have him in her life yet saddened he was confined to a future in the cartel the way she was. Because he would never know his father, the only male figures in Oscar's life would be the criminals who surrounded him growing up. The same ones who had surrounded her.

His stuffed animal lay on the floor. Walking toward the window, she scooped it up and returned it to his crib. She tucked the soft bunny in next to him, careful to hold her long brown hair back so it wouldn't fall on him.

Returning to the window, she looked out at the gardens, struck as always by how magical they appeared under the moonlight. The silvery, watery glow of green foliage mixed beautifully with the blue decorative LED lights scattered along the walking path. On cool nights, she liked to stroll the winding walkway alone and imagine she wasn't the daughter of a Colombian cartel leader.

On those nights, she would scheme of finding a way to earn a nursing degree so she could independently provide for Oscar without her father's support. She would put a little distance between her son and the cartel while still visiting her father on birthdays and holidays.

Raised voices outside the window caught her attention. The scene below was not serene. Her father and uncle were arguing, and although she couldn't hear the words, their loud statements carried heated tones. She suspected they were fighting about the same thing they always fought about—her uncle, Hermes, didn't like the way Alejandro César ran the business.

Suddenly, in one quick motion, her uncle pulled a revolver from his hip holster and fired. The loud shot rang out through the night, endlessly reverberating in her ears as her father stumbled back and fell. The man who'd always seemed dauntingly invincible to her was lying on the ground, clutching the bleeding wound in his chest.

Daniela's heart caught in her throat. A scream threatened to bubble up, but she strangled it into silence. With acres of manicured lawn on one side and the Pacific Ocean on the other, there was no one near who would hear the gunshot. No one to hear her if she screamed. Except the man holding the smoking gun which had just killed her father.

No, no. Esto no esta pasando. This is a nightmare, not reality.

She watched, frozen in place as Hermes walked over to her father, aimed at Alejandro's head, and fired again. At the harsh sound of the kill shot, Daniela jerked, bumping the curtain as she threw a hand up to her mouth.

Her uncle's head whipped up, turning in her direction even while he knelt to retrieve something out of her father's pocket. Had he seen her or caught the curtain moving from his vantage point? Regardless, Hermes had spent enough time in this house to know the precise layout. He would know by the room who had moved the curtain, and it was not the sleeping toddler.

Bile rose in Daniela's throat, burning as she stumbled backward. Her reeling mind spun into action, forcing her feet to move. She grabbed one of the toy bags off the floor and dumped out the Legos. In desperate haste, she threw in a few clothes and Oscar's favorite blanket.

After hoisting the bag on her shoulder and scooping Oscar up into her arms, she laid his sleeping head on her shoulder before running to her room. Once inside, she grabbed yesterday's clothes, carelessly strewn on a chair, along with her purse and phone, ripping charger and all out of the wall. When she scurried down the stairs, she tried not to jostle the two-year-old slumbering heavyweight, who, fortunately, hadn't woken up yet.

As she dashed toward the door leading to the garage, the back door from the garden slammed shut. Heart hammering, she never slowed as her uncle cried out, "Daniela, wait!"

Did her uncle want to talk or slow her down so he could kill her, too? She couldn't afford to hesitate and discover malicious intent. He was a cold-blooded killer—a reputation known by all the cartel and much of Colombia. He had no use for her or her son and would see them only as liabilities.

Daniela flung open the door to the garage and slammed it behind her. Oscar startled, his head coming up, wide gaze focusing on her.

The room held the faint odor of gasoline and oil, and she punched the button to open one of the six garage doors. When the automatic lights burst on overhead, she hastily grabbed the keys to her father's car from the wall mounted key rack. Thankfully, in her panic, she'd remembered her dad had taken Oscar to the zoo earlier that day, so the car seat was in his car.

The door to the garage locked from the inside, so there was no way to prevent her uncle from opening it. Looking frantically around, she spotted the heavy steel cabinet of tools the mechanic used on her father's cars. With one hand and one leg, as she still held Oscar, she shoved as hard as she could, barricading the door to the garage halfway up.

Oscar's face contorted, but she wasted no time, rushing to the vehicle and fitting him into his car seat, even as a slow fussing screech emitted from his lips. With shaking hands, she tossed the bag onto the car floor and secured his straps. By the time she sprinted around to the driver's side, sweat trickled down her face and neck.

A terrible metal screeching echoed off the walls of the garage. Her uncle was shoving all his weight against the door, moving the obstacle out of his way inch by inch. "Daniela!"

She climbed in the car, glimpsing his arm, gun in hand, stretching through the crack in the door. As she started the engine, the garage door started to close back down. A sickening sensation filled her. Her uncle had pressed the automatic garage door opener mounted on the wall.

A gun shot rang out, hitting one of the other vehicles and shattering a window. Screaming, she threw the car into drive and floored the pedal, crashing through the lower half of the descending aluminum garage door. Oscar wailed at the loud racket, but she was grateful the collision seemed to only dent the top of the car.

Heart pounding and ears ringing, she sped down the long, paved driveway. On a hard right onto the road, she fishtailed and took the dark, damp asphalt at unsafe speeds, the headlights guiding her around dizzying bends. When she was certain she wasn't being followed, she slowed to within the posted speed limit.

Oscar was still crying. She glanced at him in the rearview mirror and noted her own large brown eyes, pupils dilated with fear.

"You go ahead and cry." She let out her own long wail, which startled him. "We'll both cry and scream, because it's not fair. It's not fair!" she roared as she pounded one palm on the steering wheel.

When she finished crying, she wiped at her burning eyes with one hand, the other keeping the car straight as she tried to focus on her next course of action. They had evaded immediate danger but needed to find long-term safety.

Having relied on her father for everything, she had very little money in her own name. Now, disappearing without a chunk of cash to fund identities and travel would be impossible. She didn't have access to any of his funds. Because her father led the Colombian cartel and she didn't know who of his followers would transition their loyalty to her uncle, she had no family or friends to turn to for help. Even as she thought of a name or two who might feel compassion for her, was she willing to ask them to risk their lives?

No.

More importantly, and most terrifyingly, her uncle had been digging for a very specific device in her father's pocket. Alejandro César's encrypted text messaging device—Queen Bee. With it, Hermes could activate the César network of *Los Abajos*, her father's bees—assassins spread out around South America and the United States. With a single message, he could give a kill order. The longest anyone survived after such a message had been unleashed was two hours.

Daniela might have marginally longer than that because her uncle didn't know the passcode. Two hours or two days, she was still a dead woman. Before he could have one of the cartel's hackers reprogram Queen Bee, he could send the Four Horsemen—*los Cuartro Jinetes*. The cartel's most ruthless assassins wouldn't hesitate in killing her for a few thousand US dollars.

Oscar's future was equally bleak. Hermes could invent some tragic story about someone else killing Alejandro and Daniela and raise Oscar in the cartel as another criminal, another pawn, like how he treated his own son. Or he might not allow Oscar to live at all, fearing that if he ever found out his mother died at the hands of his great uncle, he would seek retribution.

Her next course of action hinged on how to keep Oscar safe.

She hated to think it, but there was only one place where she had any hope of survival.

Her father's murder had happened on US soil. She knew the US government would jump at the chance to put one of the Césars away. She would have to exchange testimony for her and her son's safety.

1

———

*S*ix years later...

DANIELA STIRRED the noodles on the stove, though the water wasn't boiling yet. The smell of garlic, thyme, and rosemary filled her small kitchen. She even had *torta de tres leches* made to enjoy after the spaghetti dinner. They'd had empanadas yesterday. Tonight, they were having Italian.

A new school year was underway, with Justin having entered third grade. "Honey, can you set the table?" she called to him.

He was probably playing his *Star Wars* game or watching an episode of one of the many spin-off series he liked. *The Mandalorian* or *Bad Batch* or *Clone Wars* or *Asoka*. Daniela couldn't keep up with them all.

"Five more minutes," he called back.

She smiled. He always stretched out screen time, but she couldn't be too stern, not when he made such good grades.

She pulled the salad mix out of the fridge and bumped the heavy door closed with her hip. The floor had a slight slant from warped linoleum, so the refrigerator door had a tendency to swing open if not shut firmly. The house had its quirks, but it was quiet and afforded her a pleasant environment to work from home. She could wear comfortable jeans, like now, and be here when Justin got off the bus.

After drizzling dressing into a bowl, she tossed the salad as Justin entered the kitchen. George Ezra's "Shotgun" played from her music app in the background. She loved the carefree flow of the words and the way the song conjured images of driving a convertible without a worry in the world. She swung her hips to the beat.

"Hey, Mom."

"Done defeating the evil Empire?"

"Uh, sort of. In *Star Wars Galaxy of Heroes,* you fight in teams. The goal is to collect characters and move up in rank. Not so much good versus evil." he said as he went to the fridge and poured himself a glass of milk.

She put on her best Yoda impersonation. "Hungry, you must be."

He chuckled. "Yeah."

She smiled, followed by a pang of sadness. How she longed to give him more childhood experiences, more happy memories. Mostly they did anything free—national parks, sightseeing, and free concerts. She didn't have money to take him to Disney World to see the *Star Wars* theme park. He hadn't even had a proper trip to the beach.

One day. Maybe.

She had a few thousand dollars saved, an emergency fund, and God willing she would never need it. Then she could put it toward Justin's college—her only son, once called Oscar, who was blessed to be unaware of his dark heritage.

She continued to stir the noodles, now almost boiling, and asked, "So, is that boy Mark still teasing you?"

Mark had been a nuisance last year when lunch assigned seating had landed them together. The boy would steal Justin's food or smash his sandwich and chips. Finally, after several teacher meetings, Daniela had convinced the school to separate them, only to have them land in the same classroom workstation in the third grade.

Justin shrugged in a way that told her 'yes' as he took a gulp of milk.

After dipping her wooden spoon in the simmering red sauce, she tasted it. *Needs more garlic.* "I have an idea. I'll make him a bad guy in one of the books I'm writing." She sprinkled in more seasonings and stirred.

One of her two jobs was writing serial fiction under a pseudonym and publishing stories online. Sometimes she shared her writing with Justin.

Justin gave her an inquisitive look as he sat down at the kitchen table.

"Ah, ah," she scolded lightly. "Set the table. Please and thank you."

With a groan, he pushed up and lumbered to the cabinets.

"Yes, I like that idea," she said, twirling her wooden spoon in the air as she considered writing a solution to Justin's nemesis. "He'll be a bad guy. The one who's not so competent. Like..." she turned to the fridge to fetch the Parmesan cheese as she scoured her brain for *Star Wars* references. "Who was the annoying character in Obi Wan who kept referring to himself in the third person?"

"Moralo Eval." He pulled out two plates and silverware.

"Yeah. He thought he was all that and *dulce du leche*. All ego, no real genius. I'll make Mark a character like that."

Justin chuckled.

He set the plates down, arranged the forks, spoons, and knives. "Can I play online with Chris this weekend?"

"The game where square heroes shoot square zombies?"

"They're pixelated. Not square. It's called *Intergalactic Tower Defense* on Roblox."

"Chores first. Crush cans for recycling, pick up your room, sweep floors."

"Okay. Okay."

A loud thump had Daniela jerking toward the living room window on sudden high alert. The noise was too loud to be a bird flying into the glass but not so loud to be an intruder trying to break it.

She stepped protectively in front of Justin as a figure outside the window came into view. The man had brown skin and dark, curly hair, his face contorted in a snarl.

Daniela's heart leaped into her throat.

Not this. Anything but this.

"Go bag," she croaked out to her son.

"What?"

"Go bag!" she snapped, voice and resolve stronger now. "Now, Justin."

As he ran to his room, she opened the pantry and pulled out her duffle bag from the top shelf, dropping it on the floor with a thud. She stuffed her laptop and charging cord from off the counter into it and after unzipping a side pocket, she pulled out a key. Racing to the living room, she flung open the TV console and pulled out the hidden gun box. Unlocking it, she withdrew the Beretta 418 and slipped in the clip.

"Whoa. Mom?" Justin stood, mouth agape, with a backpack slung over one shoulder.

His whole life, she'd never let him play with toy guns and abhorred violence, only to pull a weapon out in front of him now. She'd told him his 'go bag' was in case of fire, not in case of attack. She had a lot of explaining to do. Later.

"We're leaving. Stay behind me." She walked back to the kitchen, gun in hand, and picked up the duffel bag. All senses on high alert, she was surprised the attack hadn't started. If the cartel had found them, they would rain down firepower without hesitation. Maybe it wasn't them but a hooligan or a thief. She wouldn't wait around to find out.

Gun raised in a shaky hand, she opened the front door, expecting the worst. Instead, a quiet sunset greeted her, accompanied by the chirping of crickets. Music from the neighbor's three doors down wafted through the air.

Dropping her arm, she scurried to the car and opened the door for Justin. If she was overreacting and could return home, she didn't need the neighbors seeing her wielding an Italian pocket pistol. When Justin was safely inside the vehicle, she closed the door and hurried around to the driver's side, gaze snapping left and right.

Tossing the duffel in the passenger seat, she slid behind the wheel and cranked the car with fingers moist from sweat. As she pulled out of the driveway, a man stepped into view from the bushes. This wasn't the person from the window, but the sight of him—tall and lean in a dark suit—sent a wave of ice through her veins.

The cartel had found her.

Her son was in danger.

She was a dead woman.

SEBASTIAN STEPPED out of the shadows to allow Daniela to see him before she sped away, her eyes wide and terrified. She would know indisputably now that the cartel had found her. She wasn't safe, no matter how far she ran.

Jorge stumbled out after him. He'd been the klutz who'd tripped on the box bush and smacked against the window, alerting the home-owners to danger.

"Are we going after them?" Jorge asked.

"By the time we get to our car, we won't be able to catch up to them." There were few things in life worth rushing through, and this wasn't one of them.

"*Ah, hombre.*" Jorge's voice fell. "Diego will be so pissed she got away. Not to mention your father." The mouse of a man fidgeted as the stench of his perspiration filled the air. "They went through so much trouble to find her."

"She has nowhere to run to," Sebastian said calmly.

Diego Aguilar had gone to great lengths to do Hermes' bidding—working through informants and dead ends for years to finally find the retired US Marshal who'd hidden Daniela away six years ago. Diego had tracked the man down to a mountain cabin in northern California and tortured Daniela's new name out of him.

He had passed that information on to Sebastian with the promise that this was his chance at redemption with his father. Sebastian could kill the woman Hermes Cortez despised most and forever earn his father's praise.

"Where are you going?" Jorge asked, wiping at the dirt on his knees from his tumble.

In Daniela's panic, she'd left the door to the house open. Sebastian walked inside, ignoring Jorge's nervous whines, like a puppy afraid of upsetting its owner.

"Stay outside," Sebastian told him, following his nose toward the fragrant Italian seasoning floating in the air.

Daniela, this was your home, he thought.

The woman had lived in a tiny townhouse so vastly different from the luxury she'd grown up with in her father's mansions. Slipping on his leather gloves, Sebastian walked into a small kitchen where noodles boiled. He turned off the stove and pivoted slowly toward the fridge, opening the worn appliance. Inside were standard perishables —milk, sour cream, eggs, juice. A cake, untouched, sat on a middle shelf, making him wonder if they were celebrating a special occasion. He reached in and took a slice of cold pizza from a box on the second shelf. Nibbling on it, he toured the rest of the house.

The wobbly, round kitchen table would seat four, though it had only two mismatched wooden chairs. The living room held a frayed looking two-seater sofa and modest-sized flat screen TV. A stationary exercise bike in one corner was angled to face the TV. It looked second hand and beat up. He ran a gloved hand along the seat. Not a speck of dust, so she must use the machine. She had looked like she was in good shape.

He ate the pizza, chewing slowly as he continued his tour, careful not to disturb the contents of the house.

A desk between the kitchen and living room had a laptop docking station devoid of a laptop. Books about health care billing codes were stacked to one side beside a thesaurus. She worked from home, then —insurance claims, perhaps. But why a thesaurus?

Picking up her mail, he noted the name—Celeste Rivera. He

could see her as a Celeste, though did he truly know her anymore? He hadn't seen her since Oscar's first birthday party. She probably wasn't the same teenager he'd grown up knowing. He sure as hell wasn't.

Standing now in her boy's room, he scanned the decor. Oscar liked *Star Wars*, apparently, evidenced by *The Mandalorian* sheets and a green Grogu Lego figure on one shelf. Clothes were on the floor and hanging out of drawers. With such a state, how did he know which were clean and which were dirty? How did his mother know?

Sebastian had no children. Never would. He picked up a birthday card wedged in the corner of a mounted mirror. *Happy Birthday, Justin.*

So, not Oscar César but Justin Rivera.

Do you know your wicked heritage, little Justin?

If not, he soon would.

Eight was young, but when Sebastian had been that age, he'd seen his father kill a man for stealing. Better that the boy learned the evils of the world if he hadn't yet. *The earlier one hardens, the earlier one accepts the hard.* Knowing Daniela and her protective nature, she would shield her son as long as possible.

As Sebastian continued his invasion of her home and privacy, he thought of Robert Frost's *Stopping by Woods on a Snowy Evening*.

> *"Whose woods these are I think I know.*
> *His house is in the village though;*
> *He will not see me stopping here*
> *To watch his woods fill up with snow."*

Entering Daniela's bedroom, Sebastian noted the tidy efficiency of it. And the solitude.

You and I have always been alone, haven't we, dearest cousin?

They'd had each other's company and friendship for a while, but fate had sealed them in isolation. They were both outcasts, born into a family and a life they wouldn't have chosen for themselves.

He slipped open the small closet door to see a row of hanging clothes, comprising a few dresses and slacks. He ran a gloved hand along the fabric. They were worn and nothing of the classy brand names she'd once owned. The shoes were practical sneakers and sandals, except for one pair of sparkling red heels.

She'd liked her fancy heels, he recalled. She'd adored the great tales from hardship to redemption involving dazzling shoes—Cinderella's glass slipper, Dorothy's ruby slippers, Karen, from Hans Christian Andersen's *The Red Shoes*, with her magic ballerina flats.

What a strange thing to remember about someone.

He picked up the glittering red pair and carried them with him as he left her house, closing the door behind him on the way out.

A quiet life you had, Daniela.

Had she and her son been happy here? Sebastian wondered. Not that it mattered. Whatever life they'd had here was over. And when Hermes César had his way, the woman who had testified against him and put him in prison would have no life at all.

2

———

Jackson Hart crouched as he peered through the green foliage at the slender, grassy runway strip. Sweat dripped along his neck and down his spine from the quick pace he'd traversed through the jungle.

"What's the play?" Rafe Alonso asked, crouched beside Jackson and wiping at his brow.

"*Divest.* To divest someone of something is to take it away." Jackson eyed the sleek Beechcraft dual engine, looking luxuriously out of place in the belly of the jungle.

Four men were loading cellophane wrapped packages on it. Confiscating a drug runner's plane would be risky, but what choice did they have?

"This is the worst rescue mission in the history of rescue missions." The girl with them had sagged to the moist ground when Jackson and Rafe paused near the clearing.

Jackson wanted to point out how she was still alive. Instead, after two days of listening to the twenty-one-year-old's whining, he ignored her.

Sweat, filth, and bites from all manner of insects covered both of them. Jackson wanted a shower, shave, and cheeseburger, though not necessarily in that order. Fortunately, September in Colombia was favorable, with temps only in the high sixties during the day. No one was suffering from heat exhaustion after two days of hiking.

"*Divest*? I wasn't asking for the word of the day," Rafe said to him. "Are we stealing the King Air or not?"

Their plan A—rescue the millionaire's daughter and escape in the Range Rover—had been thwarted when the electrical system of their vehicle shorted, forcing them to escape on foot. A plane would put much needed distance between them and the Colombian kidnappers who were after them.

They had relayed their delay to their boss, Mica Rider, but she would be days away from organizing and implementing a second rescue. He and Rafe needed to escape the country now.

"Can you take off on that short of a runway?" Jackson asked.

Rafe smirked. "My dad and I took flying lessons from South American smugglers. This is a walk in the park."

They huddled a moment, rushing through the details as they threw a plan together.

"Sierra?" Jackson leaned toward the young woman in tattered jeans, her long blonde hair in tangles.

At least he thought it was blonde. Currently, her mop was mixed with mud and molded into thick clumps. Poor thing had been stuck in a hole in the ground for a week. He would probably be grumpy with his rescuers too if he'd been in her predicament and not yet out of danger.

"Yeah?" she asked with a weary sigh.

"Your job is to get on that plane when I give the signal."

"Okay." Sierra's tone was meeker than it had been when she'd bitched her way through the jungle.

"You got it?" Jackson's voice hardened.

"Yeah," she replied with slightly more force.

"You're sure?"

"Don't be an asshole."

Jackson smirked. That was the spitfire he wanted back at the surface before they entered danger. Pissed off was better than scared shitless.

"Let's move."

After Jackson maneuvered in place closer to the cocaine, Rafe sauntered out of the woods toward the aviators.

"*Hola, mis amigos. Estoy interesado en unirme a su carga de su avión.*" Rafe, with his bronze skin, a scar along one side of his face, and native Spanish looked like he could be one of the Colombians he approached.

If Jackson had approached them, his blond hair, blue-eyes, and American accent would have made him an immediate target. He caught part of the conversation with his weak knowledge of Spanish. Something about asking for a ride on the plane.

"*¿Qué estás haciendo aquí?*" one smuggler demanded. He wore brown cargo pants smeared with dirt, a white, sweat-stained shirt, a brown leather jacket over a white muscle shirt, and aviator glasses.

He demanded to know what Rafe was doing out here. The pilot, perhaps? Jackson wondered. Did he think he was flying for *Top Gun* with that getup?

Jackson crept over to the supply shack, leaving Sierra under the cover of ferns. The shack had shelves of tools, cans of motor oil, various mechanical parts, and dirty rags. The place smelled like a mechanic's garage.

A stack of magazines and a half full bottle of tequila sat on one shelf near a chair. Yup. Ever the optimist, the glass would always be half full for Jackson. Yet he was beginning to wonder why so many of his missions for Rider SI took dangerous turns. Maybe this was the nature of the work as a security expert, but he certainly had been kept hopping with harrowing missions so vastly different from his sleepy FBI days.

"*Mi viaje se descompuso. He estado deambulando, buscando un camino de regreso a la civilización,*" Rafe said. Because their ride had broken down. He wasn't lying.

Jackson peeked through one paneless window to see the pilot pulling his shoulders back and moving his jacket aside to reveal a holstered gun. *Yeah, yeah*, Jackson thought. *We've got guns, too.* Bunch of jackasses in the jungle with guns. Big whoop.

But the thunderous boom of gunfire would clue their pursuers onto their location, so Jackson and Rafe wanted to avoid a shootout.

Jackson soaked the oily rags with the tequila, then took a swig for himself—just enough to take the edge off his zinging nerves but not enough to impair his ability to be Rafe's copilot. As Rafe talked, Jackson stuffed the rags around the last crate of drugs.

"*Puedo pagar*," Rafe offered the men.

Now was the critical moment when the men would accept money and offer a ride, after which Rafe would negotiate transport for three passengers or the drug dealers would try to take the money. Jackson and Rafe were realistic enough to suspect the men would try to just steal the money, hence the reason Jackson was about to cause a distraction.

The pilot said, "*Las personas cuyos autos se descomponen siguen el camino de regreso a la civilización. Las personas en la clandestinidad corren el riesgo de atravesar la selva.*"

People whose cars break down follow the road back to civilization. People in hiding risk going through the jungle.

Also true.

The smugglers were no amateurs.

Jackson worked faster. Nothing would distract and terrify these men more than the threat of losing their pay day. Nothing would piss them off more, either, so guns were likely to be wielded.

Jackson was out of explosives, having used them at the kidnapping campsite. When their vehicle wouldn't start, they'd circled back around to the campsite and enacted plan B... blowing up the criminal's rides and keeping their pursuers on foot. With all of that in mind, the word of the day was most fitting. They'd *divested* the kidnappers of their victims and their pursuers of their vehicles. Now, they would *divest* the smugglers of their plane.

"*¿Es eso un no al viaje pagado?*" Rafe asked. *You don't want to get paid?*

"*Oh, nos están pagando bien.*" *We're getting paid, all right.*

Jackson lit the rags on fire, and in seconds, pandemonium broke loose. Rafe lunged for the distracted pilot, who'd turned to gape at the flames and smoke. At the same instant, Jackson leapt from behind the crate, fists swinging. He landed a solid punch to the face of the largest of the two smugglers.

As the man stumbled back, his colleague reached for an AK-47 propped against the wheel of the plane. Jackson pounced on him before the man's fingers touched metal. He rammed a knee into his flank, bringing the man to his knees with the agonizing blow to his kidneys.

The first man recovered, and from his peripheral vision, Jackson witnessed him pulling his handgun. Jackson ducked and spun as the man fired. When the bullet sank into the steel of the plane, Jackson hoped it had hit nothing critical to the plane's ability to take off and remain airborne.

As he pivoted, Jackson swept the AK-47 into his grip and raised the muzzle toward the man with the handgun. Before he could fire, Sierra appeared behind the man and hit him over the head with the tequila bottle with the force of a woman unleashing a week's worth of pent-up rage.

Jackson sighed in begrudging admiration. The girl didn't follow orders well, but she had spared him from killing a man who was about to kill him. Though he went into every mission knowing he had a client—and himself—to defend, he'd never killed anyone, and preferred not to start today.

"In the plane," he ordered.

As she dropped the empty bottle and bolted for the entrance, he picked up the fallen man's gun and scanned the scene. The pilot was on the ground face down, eating dirt, successfully neutralized by Rafe, who was now tucking into the cockpit. A million dollars of drugs burned in billows of sickly black smoke. The toxic odor reeked of mixed scents reminiscent of nail salon chemicals and burning tires. The other smuggler was shoving to his knees.

Jackson put the muzzle of the AK-47 against his head. "*Quédate abajo.*" *Stay down,* he commanded.

The man complied, face down in the dirt, and Jackson raced to the entry, scrambled up the steps, pulled the stairs up, and secured the door.

Sierra huddled in the back by the cargo.

"Strap in," he told her, flipping the safety on the automatic weapon and stowing it and the handgun in the back.

As he climbed up front, Rafe was finishing his preflight check. "What part of a quiet take over confused you?" Rafe asked, checking gauges.

"Meh. By the time we had shots fired, the smoke from the burning coke was a half mile high, announcing our whereabouts anyway."

Rafe glanced irritably at Jackson with a shake of his head. When he pushed up the throttle but kept a foot on the brake, the engine roared even as they remained motionless. Rafe adjusted the flaps.

"This is a nicer plane than I would have expected," Jackson commented, swallowing back his fear at seeing the short runway in front of them.

Lots of lift, little drag, Jackson hoped, staring ahead at the tiny airstrip. The engine's whine grew louder.

"These old models are popular for drug running," Rafe said. "Longer distances than single engine Cessnas, though those are frequently used too." He sniffed. "You smell like alcohol."

"Tequila. And you're welcome."

"I'd be thanking you if you'd saved any for me."

"You can't drink and fly."

As the plane lurched forward, Jackson gripped the dash. The plane gained speed rapidly, the end of the runway precariously approaching.

"Trees." Jackson pointed out. "Trees," he repeated, voice an octave higher.

"Yup. Trees." Rafe acknowledged, calmly pulling back on the yoke.

At what seemed like the last possible second, Rafe lifted the plane, missing an impact with the jungle wall. When Jackson glanced out the window, armed men emerged from the tree line, pointing at the plane.

Disaster averted.

They could get the client's daughter to safety.

SEBASTIAN STEPPED into the visitation room, suppressing the urge to shudder at the sight of the bars and bland walls of the prison. He would wither and die in a place like this. His mind drifted again to Robert Frost.

> *My little horse must think it queer*
> *To stop without a farmhouse near*
> *Between the woods and frozen lake*
> *The darkest evening of the year.*

His father sat chained to the table at the San Quentin State Prison. He wore an orange jumpsuit and a perpetual frown. His nose was crooked—rumor claimed Alejandro had broken it more than once in their shared childhood. Now, Hermes had leathery skin scoured by a roadmap of wrinkles over his face and arms, which had lost muscle tone as he'd aged. Despite that, he was still a formidable man with a formidable ability to scowl people into submission. Building and maintaining the cartel beside his brother, Hermes was no stranger to physical hardship and had no qualms in delivering physical hardship upon others—even his only son.

"Diego tells me you had someone dear to me in your sights," Hermes said, voice a menacing, gravely sound.

Sebastian unbuttoned his Brioni suit jacket and slid into the seat across from him. "We found her home." He was prepared to have this conversation in part riddles because the prison had eyes and ears.

"Then why am I not hearing how she's convening with Our Heavenly Father?"

Sebastian sniffed, detesting the mingling smells of body odor from the inmates, cheap cologne from the guard, and stale cigarettes from both. "Jorge stumbled in the dark, made a ruckus, and tipped her off. She had a go bag ready and fled."

Fled with her son, Sebastian thought.

"Jorge? You took the most incompetent accomplice for this? You disgrace me."

"We were just confirming our intel. I would have gone back with Diego to take out the trash."

Unlike his father, all heated temper, Sebastian was icy calm. His father would have preferred they attack with guns blazing in a take-no-prisoners massacre, but Sebastian was more methodical. His tactics meant he was still alive with all of his limbs six years into running drugs for his incarcerated father.

"Track her down," Hermes demanded.

"Me?" Sebastian's cool composure threatened to crack. He didn't track people down. This wasn't part of his role. Daniela was an exception. "I'm overseeing—"

"Give that to someone else. Do this job for me. Quickly, before she goes to ground."

"But—"

"Stop being a pansy." His face contorted, making his bent nose look more prominent. "You lost her, you'll fix it. Tell me you'll do this."

Sebastian ground his teeth together. "I'll do this."

"Was there a man with her at her home?"

Thinking back to her house, Sebastian recalled no evidence of a lover—no pictures or clothes, or second toothbrush. "No."

"A woman always runs to a man. Find what man she would run to, and you will find her."

At his father's dismissive tone, Sebastian stood. When he looked down at Hermes, still seated, Sebastian could almost imagine he felt pity for the bitter man, whose thirst for vengeance ate at his very sanity. Sebastian could almost fool himself into thinking he was no longer intimidated by the father who'd beaten and bruised him as a child in an attempt to make him tougher.

Almost.

3

———————

*D*aniela drove through the night along the interstate, thinking about her destination while Justin slept. He'd wept when she told him there would be no going back to his school and his friends. He'd been angry and hurt when she'd explained The United States Federal Witness Protection Program (WITSEC) to him and why they'd been in it... and why, now, they were unable to remain in hiding.

In a matter of minutes, the life Justin had known had been shattered, much the way hers had when her father had been murdered. She'd wanted so much to give him a happy, shielded childhood, and her heart ached for the emotional pain he was suffering. She felt as though she had failed as a mother, even though she wasn't responsible for the cartel finding them.

Should she have told him the truth sooner? She hadn't wanted him to feel different from his childhood peers or burden him with the secrets of his heritage. Instead, she had created a protective illusion around Justin, and the illusion had just burst.

As Justin stewed in silence and she kept the car heading East, her mind contemplated the plan she had schemed over the course of years. She'd often thought about what she would do should the cartel ever find her.

But she couldn't enact her plan without help.

Although she didn't have her father's resources or deviousness, she had his resolve. She would seek help from one of the few men from her life before WITSEC, who'd been kind to her. She hoped he would help and still had the chivalrous streak she'd glimpsed long ago. Would he even remember the first night they'd met?

As she drove, mesmerizing lights on the highway zipping past her, she thought of the first time she'd met the man in whom she was now contemplating placing her faith.

EIGHT YEARS AGO, she'd sat on the carpet near the banister overlooking the living room, with her dress tucked around her and sparkling blue heels resting beside her. Her father hosted wonderful parties, and she'd seen them all from the banister—in this house and the one in Colombia.

Below her, the partygoers had flirted and gossiped while devouring champagne and caviar like there was no tomorrow. Music, laughing, and sounds of frolicking had filled the air, all a dance and courtship of sorts before many of them would slink off to private rooms and not-so-private corners for more intimate encounters. She observed the scene like the captivated spectator of a movie, dreaming of a day when she could be part of the festivities. And yet, somehow, she knew she never would be.

She was a sheltered virgin—eighteen and still a girl. Few men in her father's circle would risk his wrath and venture to court her. Fewer still were men she would consider safe or trustworthy for a romantic interlude.

A man joined her on the floor and crossed his legs as he sat. She eyed him, not recognizing him as one of her father's friends or many employees. She would've remembered that face. He had radiant blue eyes, strong cheekbones, a narrow nose, and a firm jaw. Full blond hair was neatly combed and parted. In his shiny blue suit and black

Gucci loafers, he looked like something out of a GQ magazine. She glanced around him, trying to figure out if he'd joined her or somebody else, but they were the only two people up here.

"Enjoying the party?" he asked, tone all easy North American without a particular accent, though her exposure to US citizens was limited.

"They're always amazing. Gorgeous people with gorgeous bodies."

His lips curved. "That wasn't much of an answer."

"I enjoy them from up here. That's about it." She looked away, uncomfortable at the way her body responded warmly to his light smile.

"So why not go down there? You're missing out on the champagne."

She frowned. Aside from being underage—which had stopped no one in her family—she didn't drink champagne because alcohol gave her the munchies. Her father, aunts, and uncles were always telling her how she needed to lose weight, but she wouldn't explain that to this stranger. Instead of an answer, she shrugged her shoulders.

"I'm Jackson."

"Daniela. I don't recognize you as one of my father's usual guests."

He smiled, a full set of white teeth. "It's my first time at an Alejandro César party."

She tried to gauge his age. Twenty-five maybe.

"What type of work do you do?" As soon as she asked, she feared the answer. If he was here and not one of her father's employees, then Jackson was one of the many people who wanted to get in bed with her father for business. She didn't want to know if that was the case, because she didn't want this handsome American with the amiable smile to be one of *them*.

"I'm an escort."

Daniela giggled, covering her mouth to keep the noise down, even though no one would overhear them with the music blaring downstairs.

"What?" His smile widened. "I don't look good enough to be one?

I wore my sexiest suit tonight." He played at straightening his lapels as he feigned insult.

"*Verdadero*?" Was he serious? She'd known that some men in her family weren't above bringing hookers to these parties, but it hadn't occurred to her that someone might bring a man.

"That's my date." He pointed to a woman sitting on the couch with one leg draped over Daniela's second cousin's thigh.

They were drinking champagne, and the woman was laughing while doting excessively on him. Daniela suspected the deep pockets of the cartel had this woman fawning over her second cousin, rather than the man's witty comments.

"As you can see, my services are not currently needed." Jackson didn't sound offended.

"Well, if it's any consolation, on a scale of one to ten, you're a ten and he's a two. She's an idiot to not be with you."

Jackson's eyes sparkled. "Thank you. It is a consolation to hear that."

He shifted his weight, bumping knees with her. "So, which one of these men are you dating, and why isn't he up here with you?"

"I don't have a boyfriend, or a date. Look at the women they have to choose from. Why would they choose me?" She regretted the words the instant they left her mouth. She wasn't looking for pity and certainly didn't want false flattery from anyone. "Besides, my father is Alejandro César. Everyone's scared to death of him." Even if she sparked a man's interest, he wouldn't dare try to date her.

"Oh, that's unfortunate. But it means you get to watch nice parties. And I bet you use that fancy pool out back when no one is around." He lowered his voice to a conspiratorial hush.

She grinned. "Definitely. But it also means I'm a little trapped when I think about what I want to do with the rest of my life. I always have to put ambitions in the context of what the rest of my family does." Wow, Jackson was easy to talk to. Maybe that was a skill escorts possessed. It definitely made him more desirable.

"Do you? How old are you?" he asked.

"Eighteen."

His throat bobbed slightly in a swallow, but his expression stayed soft. "Your father will let you go to college, right? You can pick the career you want and be the person you want to be. Nobody can force you to do what they do. And a good father wouldn't ask you to."

She liked that his words were filled with compassion, but they also showed how little he knew about the cartel.

"I don't know. I'm a liability."

"What do you mean?"

"My father tells me he keeps me close because his enemies might take me away or hurt me to get to him." She glanced warily at Jackson. Her father was always warning her about spies. "I don't think he'd let me go away to school," she continued. "I've been home-schooled all my life." She ran a finger over a sparkling rhinestone on her heels, uncomfortable with how easily she opened up to this stranger.

Did Jackson have an agenda in speaking with her? She didn't want to think so, but how did one spot a spy? She would simply tell him nothing of value and not risk spilling secrets.

Jackson was silent, though he conveyed empathy without words as he slid a hand over and brushed her fingers, stopping their fidgeting on her shoes. Tantalizing sparks dance along her bare skin from his touch.

"Why do you do what you do?" she asked.

He raised his shoulder in a half shrug. "The money's decent. But I also get my internal reward by helping people. I'm pretty good at making people feel good about themselves. Sometimes they just need someone to talk to."

She snorted. "I can't argue with that. If I could be anything I wanted to be, I'd be a nurse. That's how I'd help people."

"So, be a nurse. Be what you want to be."

"That simple, huh?"

"As simple as walking down there and joining the party."

"I'm not really the right size for these types of parties." *Gah!* She should stop talking. She sounded like a spoiled child craving attention. In truth, she knew what paid for these parties. This wasn't

Cinderella's ball in front of the bars she watched through. This was drugs and sex, paid for with drugs and sex. Even if she fit in by appearances, she wouldn't join on principal.

Jackson was silent for so long, she turned to look at him. He made steady, direct eye contact with her and leaned closer. His heated gaze had her pulse quickening.

He leaned closer. "You honestly don't know how beautiful you are, do you?" he asked, warm breath caressing her skin.

She stared at him, puzzled, and tried to find some trace of irony or disdain. But only those lovely topaz eyes stared back at her, heating her blood to unprecedented levels. "You're serious?"

He traced a finger down her bare shoulder beside her spaghetti strap dress. "I am very serious. And if this is the first time you're hearing it, then I'm sorry you live in a toxic environment. You deserve better." He brushed his lips ever so slightly on her bare shoulder, causing warmth to pool in her core. He straightened. "I've never been paid for sex in my entire life. And I wouldn't start now. I'm telling you, you're beautiful because you are, not because I'm trying to get in bed with you."

She gaped at him. So, he was an actual escort—a paid date—and not a prostitute. That brought some relief, but she wanted him to try to get in bed with her.

His mouth curved into a smile, making her wonder if he knew the effect he had on her body.

"That being said, I wouldn't turn you down if you were offering."

Her heart thudded as the room grew warm. She turned away from his hungry gaze to look out over the crowd. The urge to be reckless and carefree welled inside her.

Be what you want to be.

At this moment, she wanted to be a beautiful woman in Jackson's arms.

She bit her bottom lip. "I am offering," she blurted, turning to look at him again.

His eyes widened in surprise as his breath hitched. Then he

smiled as if he was both surprised and nervously delighted. Only in her fantasies had a man ever been delighted to lie with her.

Here was a gorgeous man she'd never seen making a gorgeous offer she might never receive again. When she stood, heels in hand, he stood. She slipped her free hand into his and led him down the hall. Would anyone notice her slipping out? *Oh, silly girl, definitely not.*

Her heart was racing now—terrified and exhilarated all at once—but she wouldn't let herself second-guess her decision. She wanted this more than she wanted her next breath.

She didn't know if intimacy would be magical the way it seemed to be in all the Nora Roberts books she'd read or if it would be brief and rough and over. But Jackson held her hand lightly and gave her hope he would handle her with care. He had so far. It could've all been a ruse, but his compliments felt genuine.

When they reached her bedroom, she closed and locked the door. Jackson leaned down and gave her a tender kiss. Her first real kiss. Her first real everything. Even as her head spun as if she'd gulped a bottle of champagne, she steadied her resolve to go through with this.

"Will someone check on you?" Jackson asked.

"No. No one checks on me." The elation in her voice surprised her. "And my father is busy conducting business," she added.

The next kiss was less chaste, but Jackson was still tender as he eased her lips open with his tongue, exploring and coaxing. Passion sprang from her like water from a geyser. Her whole body tingled with anticipation.

"You can tell me to stop anytime," he said, voice wonderfully husky.

"Okay."

"I won't hurt you."

"I know."

His hands skimmed over her shoulders and down her arms before finding their way to the zipper on the back of her dress...

.   .   .

Sirens speeding past her car snapped Daniela out of her memory. The police cruiser was heading in the other direction. She glanced at Justin in the backseat, who slept.

Daniela couldn't run forever. After just these few days, she was a wreck. She knew where she needed to go and who she needed to ask for help. But she didn't know if he was the same man she'd known or if she could trust him.

"Honey, I'm home." Jackson let himself inside his house and reset his alarm. His voice echoed through the empty space, and his chuckle that followed was slightly bitter.

No one waited to greet him after his work trips. Heck, even when he'd been married during his FBI days, no one had affectionately greeted him when he'd arrived home. He and his now ex-wife had been ships passing in the night.

Would he have to accept the possibility that this was his life? He loved his work at Rider Security and Investigation—bodyguard and retrieval specialist—and the men and women he worked with were like family, but time alone carried an aching hollowness.

Speaking of ache. The jungle rescue, followed by hours of cramped travel in planes, had left him sore. He would jog it out, followed by that juicy cheeseburger he'd been craving since eating dehydrated meals on the go in Colombia. He could have settled for fast food or a restaurant burger, but he wanted homemade—juicy, extra cheese, and a butter toasted bun.

He stripped out of his jeans and pulled on running shorts before calling Rafe.

When Rafe answered, Jackson said cheerfully, "I'm firing up the grill tonight. Want to come over for cheeseburgers? Watch a game?"

"Ah, sorry, man," Rafe said. "Dia is coming to visit."

Jackson considered extending the invitation to Rafe's girlfriend. That would make him a third wheel, but he could manage it.

"Along with Santino and Ava," Rafe added, tone apologetic.

Jackson definitely couldn't be a fifth wheel to the twin brothers and their love interests.

Solo cheeseburger. Check.

"No worries, man. Have a great time." He disconnected the call. Firing up the grill for one person seemed like an excessive use of biomass fuel, even if he made his a double. Undeterred, he decided he'd do smash burgers on the kitchen griddle. The meat wouldn't have that smoky flavor but would hold more moisture.

Aside from a few fleeting date nights, cooking for himself had been his norm since his divorce. Dating with his bizarre schedule—leaving on short notice to fulfill a client's needs—was challenging. Sometimes jobs were weeks or months long on protection duty. If over half the Rider team hadn't seemed to meet their match, he might have stopped believing in couples finding happy existences together, especially in his line of work.

Maybe he would find that special spark with someone.

Maybe he already had, and he'd missed his opportunity forever.

4

---

*M*ica Rider, owner of Rider Security and Investigation, sat at her desk, rummaging through email updates from her bodyguards on or recently on assignments in the field.

Rafe and Jackson had arrived home no worse for wear after a harrowing escape in Colombia. Ryan and Reece were safely delivering Sierra Cavendish back to her parents, who seemed like the type to have the good sense to get the girl some post-traumatic stress counseling. She'd been an excelling college student with a fencing scholarship before her vacation in South America turned into a kidnapping. Hopefully, she could mentally recover and enjoy life again.

Mica was leaning back, running fingers through her loose blond curls to massage her scalp, when Claire poked her head into her office.

"I have a tranq dart prototype to show you."

"Great. Let's have a look." Mica stood and followed Claire to her office.

Claire was the company's information technologist, mission coordinator, gadget guru, and hacker. Her slender body was covered in her usual loose cotton shirt and yoga pants, her black bob swaying as she walked.

When they reached Claire's office, Mica noted the woman had tidied her usual clutter. Instead of the twinkling fairy lights around the ceiling, she had strips of neon LED lights. The room's vibe had transformed from magical fairy land to hacker/gamer cavern. The desk was still overloaded with five large monitors.

Claire lifted the dart from a small side table and pointed to each segment. "So, basics. Needle. Drug. Air pressure chamber. Over the hole in the needle's side is this little rubber stopper. When the pointy end hits the target at fifty feet per second, the needle punctures the skin, the stopper is pushed back, and the drug is forced out through the now exposed hole by the air pressure in the chamber."

"Very cool."

Claire set down the dart and picked up the gun. "Here's the wicked part. Standard tranquilizer guns use air pressure and fire a single round. You pull back to cock it, like a Nerf gun. More sophisticated ones used CO_2, like a paintball gun."

"This is definitely a more sophisticated one."

Claire always created or found the best gadgets.

"Of course." Claire beamed, holding the sleek black gun. "This is an aluminum, gas-based pistol with a six chamber rotating barrel. It's a Bill Sharp prototype, so not on the market."

Mica held the gun manufactured by Sharp Industries. "This is different from what Shoup's men used." The Rider SI adversary had mercenaries carrying tranquilizer guns for abductions. After they'd swiped one during a skirmish, she wanted to create something similar as a means of nonlethal attack.

"Correct. His was single shot."

"Range?"

"Five to thirty meters. There are long-range ones, but they use a longer barrel, which means they aren't practical for conceal carry. Other issues to consider... this won't penetrate thick clothing, certainly not Kevlar. This is dosed for a seventy-kilogram man—theoretically, since I can't really test it on people. If you have a small person, there's risk the dose could be lethal."

"I feel like none of our enemies are little."

"Right. Most are ex-military or big-ol' criminals. With that in mind, it may take two darts to really put someone down. If they're a daily drinker or drug user—and therefore have conditioned their body for a higher tolerance—these may not work at all. If the person shot is severely allergic to something we used in the mixture, he or she could suffer an anaphylactic reaction and die."

"Lots of limitations," Mica said, running a hand through her short blonde waves. "I'm guessing Shoup never lost sleep over these pesky lethal issues when he authorized his men to use these."

Claire snorted. "Not likely. Another limitation—effects won't be instantaneous like in the movies."

"Got it." Mica's pursuit of nonlethal weapons had yet to produce the ideal solution.

Claire pointed to the bright blue liquid in the syringe. "And this cocktail contains prescription grade drugs. Because none of our operatives have a medical license, there are legal implications if we're caught. Well, even if they did have a medical license, shooting this into someone—and thereby administering medication without consent—would result in a loss of license and, again... legal implications."

Mica smirked. "So does shooting people with real bullets. You'll make sure your prints aren't on any of these darts?"

"Of course."

Mica inspected one of them. "Why is the medication blue?"

Claire gave a sheepish smile. "Technically, the concoction comes out clear, but I added a little blue food coloring because it looks cooler."

Claire's watch buzzed, and she jerked her arm up to read the small screen. "Code Silver in the elevator."

"Sh-sugar." Mica dashed down the hallway to her office. She shrugged on her shoulder holster, reached into her drawer, and withdrew her 9mm. As she crossed the room, she slid the gun into the holster.

Claire snatched up her electronic tablet and began pulling up a visual from the elevator camera onto one of her screens.

"How many?" Mica asked.

"Um." Claire stepped in line behind her. "Well, one packing. There are two people coming up."

With escalating threats to Rider team members, Mica had a gun detector installed on the elevator. The software hid behind the walls and used low frequency radar combined with machine learning technology to generate a probability of a concealed weapon and its type. When they weren't working here, they had an off-site unlisted office only Rider employees knew how to access where they didn't have to worry about uninvited guests.

Mica turned and headed down the hallway, Claire in tow. When they reached the end of the hall and the closed door leading to the Rider lobby, Mica stopped.

The elevator dinged open.

The monitor videoing the lobby showed a woman with a suitcase, a satchel, and a duffel bag. Beside her stood a boy of about eight, holding her hand.

"Which one is armed?" Mica whispered, relaxing slightly at the sight of a mother and son who obviously looked scared.

Claire glanced at the screen of the tablet she held. "Mom. AI says satchel."

Mica nodded, reassured the gun was not somewhere the woman could immediately access. If artificial intelligence kept her team safer, she would use it.

When the holographic image of a receptionist behind the desk greeted the guests, the mother looked like she might bolt. She didn't appear to be someone who'd come here for a fight. She had smooth, light-bronze skin and long brown hair—perhaps central or South American in her heritage. The boy had lighter skin and lighter brown hair, trimmed around the ears. His eyes were a startling bright blue.

"Stay hidden. Stay listening."

"Always," Claire said, slipping back down the hallway.

Mica opened the door and stepped through, giving the woman a welcoming smile. "Hi, I'm Mica Rider."

The nervous woman's eyes darted to the gun in Mica's holster, but Mica didn't cover it. The prospective client had come to Mica's office carrying a concealed weapon, so Mica would make sure hers was readily available. Rider SI took the possibility of threats seriously.

"How can I help you?" Mica asked when the woman didn't reciprocate by giving her name.

"I need to hire your services. And I can pay." Her accent was light, like maybe a hint of Latina washed out by more Midwestern American.

She tossed the small duffle bag at Mica's feet. The zipper was open, and prepaid credit cards filled it.

Mica recognized a woman on the run. Abusive ex? Diabolical employer?

Knowing the Rider team's propensity to attract clients with complicated predicaments, Mica's instincts told her this woman's problem would contribute to Mica's sleepless nights.

She stepped aside and gestured to the doorway. "Why don't you come into our conference room and tell me about your situation?"

DANIELA FOLLOWED MICA, but when the blonde woman, who was maybe mid-thirties, didn't touch the duffel bag, she gestured for her son to pick it up.

"My name is Cele—"

No. She was done hiding. She would use her real name, not her WITSEC name. "Daniela. And this is Justin." She would use her son's assigned name because he'd been too young to remember the name his grandfather had given him. Justin was the name he knew—at least he could keep that part of himself. Besides, she was fond of this one, as she'd been able to choose it for him.

They walked down a hallway and past offices and a large exercise area before turning into a conference room with a rectangular table, a monstrous flat screen monitor mounted on one wall.

"Please have a seat. Can I get you something to drink?" Mica offered.

"Coffee and a water would be wonderful. Thank you."

Mica nodded and sat, making no motion to get the beverages she'd offered.

She glanced at Daniela's suitcase. "You have a place to stay?"

"No." Daniela slid into one of eight chairs, feeling the comfort of the chair and some of her anxiety about surviving the trip here wane. "But we can find somewhere."

"We'll work on that. We can arrange a hotel where the reservation won't be under your name or any aliases you might have. How long have you been on the run?"

Damn, this woman was perceptive. Her insight was unnerving but also oddly reassuring, as though perhaps detecting such things translated into excelling at security.

Daniela smiled wearily. "Sometimes it feels like six years, but we spent all of that in witness protection. Justin and I have technically been on the run for three days."

"WITSEC?" Mica's eyes widened. "Does your marshal know where you are?"

"I hope not."

Mica's brows furrowed and her expression turned shrewd. "Why is that?"

Daniela placed a protective hand on Justin's shoulder. "Someone leaked our identities, and men came after us. Who do you trust after something like that? Who do you trust when you have to save your son's life? Not the people employed to protect you. And my experience with the US government isn't one that garners confidence. If I sought refuge with them after the attack, they would have wasted time accusing me of being the leak and asking who I contacted from my past before they looked in the mirror."

Despite her testimony, Daniela had never been treated like an unfortunate victim and witness to events outside of her control.

Marshals had treated her like the daughter of a drug dealer who might as well be a criminal herself.

Mica glanced at Justin as if she wanted to ask Daniela something sensitive but thought better of it in front of her son.

"I will tell you what I told my son." Daniela ran a hand through Justin's hair, a knot forming in her stomach.

He'd been savvy enough to understand the parallels in the story, and he'd been angry, then cried in her arms. Today, he'd been mostly melancholy, resigned to a fate neither of them could control. Every time she looked at the despair in his eyes, her heart broke all over again.

She leaned back and crossed her legs. "Let me tell you a tale, Mica Rider. It's not a Disney fairytale, more like something out of the Grimm Brothers. Once upon a time, there was a young princess, locked away in a tower of fortune under the watchful eye of a king. This was no benevolent king, but one who earned his riches through the conquest and misery of others. He stashed the princess away for his safety, not her own. Despite that, her life was one of luxury, which few children have. Yet, the only thing she wanted was her father's love."

The conference room door opened and a woman of about thirty with a sleek black bob entered with water and a tray containing coffee, sugar, and cream.

"This is our tech support, Claire. Claire, this is Daniela and Justin."

Claire set down the beverage tray.

"Thank you," Daniela said.

"Hey, nice to meet you. Way to rock the TIE fighter t-shirt." Claire fist-bumped Justin before she backed out of the conference room, closing the door behind her.

He grinned in the first semblance of a happy emotion Daniela had seen from him in three days. She wanted to pull him into her arms, but she needed to relay her history to Mica.

Daniela continued her tale as she added cream to her coffee from small, peel back cups. "Then, one day, a handsome prince charmed his way into the princess's life. And he gave her the greatest gift she never knew she wanted." Daniela paused and stroked a hand through Justin's light brown hair. Her heart warming, she smiled before turning her gaze back to Mica. "The birth of his first grandson brought the king much joy. He became… not good, but we'll say less ruthless. His behavioral changes improved his relationship with his daughter but made him weak in the eyes of his family, who thirsted for the throne. One dreadful night, amidst a heated argument, the king's brother killed the king, and his daughter was the only witness. After the princess agreed to testify, she was forced into hiding with her son."

"Daniela César," Mica said breathlessly. "I remember the stories in the news. That was…"

"Six years ago." Daniela nodded. "I'm Daniela Rivera now."

"And you want protection through us?"

"No. I want freedom," she said firmly, leaning forward, one hand fisted on the table. "I don't know how, but I don't want to hide anymore." She pointed a finger down on the table. "And I'm going to tell you exactly who on your team will help me."

5

---

*J*ackson exited the elevator, pressed his thumbprint to the electric locking mechanism, and opened the door leading to the Rider offices.

After he and Rafe had escaped the jungle and transferred the client's daughter to Reece and Ryan for safe travel home, Jackson had taken the longest, hottest bath of his life and eaten the biggest, sloppiest cheeseburger he could fit in a bun. Thank goodness for first world amenities. Then, he'd waited restlessly for his next assignment.

Mica had summoned him into the office by a text message with no details about the next case. Of course, he had no doubt the task would be interesting. He'd loved his job since joining the team and had fast made friends with everyone with whom he'd worked.

As he walked down the hall, he paused outside the exercise room, his gaze snagging on the sight of a boy seated on the mat, playing with a set of magnetic building shapes. He looked to be about eight, and as far as Jackson recalled, no one working for Rider had a child that age.

A client's child, perhaps?

He didn't like the idea of someone with a child being in the type of trouble that would require Rider SI. Bristling, he prepared himself to tell Mica he'd be happy for any assignment to keep a kid safe. He'd enjoyed protecting the Sizani family over the summer with Rafe, despite some harrowing close calls.

When Jackson entered the conference room, the sight of the brunette in the chair stopped his heart. "Daniela."

"Well, that certainly seems to verify your story," Mica said to Daniela. Mica wore her gun in a holster—unusual because she didn't arm herself for meetings with clients. Her short stature and attractive features with platinum blond hair could mislead someone into thinking she was harmless. The woman didn't need a gun to take someone down, but there the weapon was for all to see.

Daniela stood. Her hair was shorter, though still long, and she was thinner, but with the same soft skin and decadent chocolate eyes he'd lost himself in—more than once. She wore stain-washed jeans, a purple t-shirt, and a pair of frayed boat shoes.

The child had grown into a boy, still entertained by the magnetic building toys Jackson had gifted him.

"Special Agent Hart." Daniela's cheeks flushed as she tightly gripped the back of the chair she stood behind.

"It's just Jackson now." But she must already know that. "You're here." Joy at seeing her mixed with dread at what her status out of hiding might mean.

"I need your help." She glanced at Mica. "Help from all of you." Her Latina accent, once prominent, was now barely noticeable.

Jackson looked at Mica, whose expression turned grim. "She's the new client?" he asked.

"Possibly," Mica said, caution in her voice.

Unlike her to be noncommittal, Jackson thought. She usually researched clients before meetings and had already decided to decline or accept their case prior to in-person conferences.

"What happened to WITSEC?" He turned back to Daniela.

"Someone came after Justin and me. I don't trust them anymore."

Justin. Her son's WITSEC name. Jackson hadn't known that. And who had Daniela been for the past six years? A single mom living in fear of discovery. Or not single? Witnesses in protection weren't forced into celibacy. And Jackson certainly hadn't been, though he'd had little sexual appetite since his divorce.

"We'll help you," he said.

"Jackson," Mica warned.

"We'll help you," he repeated.

Of course they would. Mica didn't turn away anyone in need. Case in point—himself needing a rewarding job. And based on past cases, Rider didn't back away from challenges. Besides, Jackson had let Daniela go twice in the last eight years. He wouldn't walk away a third time. Never again.

Although he didn't believe in fate or destiny, he couldn't deny something had brought them back together. He felt the urge to seize the chance to stay in her life this time. But that may be as impossible as it had been the last time they'd parted ways.

"Will you excuse us a moment?" Mica smiled politely at Daniela before shooting daggers at Jackson.

They stepped into the hallway together, and Mica closed the conference room door.

She was a foot shorter than him, but height differences didn't stop her from going nose to nose with him. "You need to get your head in the game." She jabbed a finger into his chest. "You don't go around blindly agreeing *my team* to a client."

Shit. He'd never seen Mica so angry. He couldn't jeopardize his job, but he also wouldn't turn Daniela away.

He started to open his mouth, but Mica wasn't done. "Do you even know what she's asking? Because it's not as simple as delivering her back to WITSEC. She wants a plan to get her out of hiding, and something that ludicrous will be dangerous."

Jackson swallowed.

"Yeah. Now you've got the right facial expression." Mica ran a hand through her ear-length blonde hair as she turned away, paused, and pivoted back to face him. "What is she to you? You love her? Is she part of the reason you left the FBI?"

"No. I don't know." He didn't even know who Daniela was anymore... or ever. After only two amazing nights together, he couldn't claim to love her. "My reason for leaving the FBI is the same as I told you when you hired me. The Bureau knew nothing about Daniela and me beyond office speculation and gossip."

"Is she a threat to you?" Mica asked.

"Daniela? No. Why would you ask?" His gaze rested on Mica's gun, the one she never wore to meet new clients.

"She has a weapon with her, which I presumed was for her own safety, until she told me the story of you two. A woman raising a man's son by herself might harbor a grudge. Especially if she has Alejandro César's ruthless blood coursing through her veins. A woman like that might decide the absentee father of her son needs to be dealt with."

"Wh—what?" The room swayed beneath Jackson's feet as he shook his head. "No. She told me he wasn't mine." His chest tightened, and he felt like he was trying to breathe underwater. He placed a hand against the hallway wall to steady himself. "When she went into WITSEC, she explicitly said he wasn't mine."

"*Sonofasnowshoe*," Mica pseudo swore. "I put the pieces together when she asked specifically for your help, but I didn't think to ask her if you knew." Mica grit her teeth. "You can't look into that kid's face and tell me he's not yours. He has your eyes, Jackson."

Keeping one hand on the wall to hold himself up, he backed slowly down the hallway with shaking knees, pausing at the opening to the gym room where the boy played on the mat.

After a moment, he looked up at Jackson with a pair of blue eyes. "Hi."

Jackson's heart raced as his mouth went dry. "Hi. Those look like fun."

The boy shrugged, setting the house he'd built down on the floor. "Where's my mom?"

"We were just chatting. She's in the conference room. Maybe we'll all grab lunch together." A lump in Jackson's throat refused to ease.

"Okay." The boy turned back to his structure—a two-story block house with triangular pieces for the roof.

Mica came up beside Jackson and whispered, "I need to know if this woman is a threat to you."

This was his boss. The choices he'd made in his past were presenting as danger from a drug cartel, and Mica was protecting him. In the Bureau's eyes, he would have been violating the number one rule: *don't embarrass the Bureau.* Rather than expelling him to deal with his family issues on his own, Mica was treating him like family. The Rider team protected their own.

He shook his head in response to her question before tearing his gaze from the boy. Although Daniela had lied to him, he didn't think she had a mean bone in her body. "If she's asking for help, then that's what she wants. She wouldn't manipulate her way in here to get to me." Time and hardships could have changed her, but he doubted the change would be drastic enough for her to become a threat. If he was wrong about her character, he would accept the consequences.

Mica nodded resolutely.

He walked with her back toward the conference room. Outside the door, he hesitated. In a soft, dry, raspy voice, he told Mica, "I didn't know he was mine." Daniela had lied to him, which somehow felt like a failure on his part.

"Now that you know, what are you going to do about it?"

"Help them. Please, Mica, can we help them?" Alone, he was no match for the cartel. He needed the resources and hive mind of the Rider team.

She sucked in a deep breath. "We'll help them."

DANIELA PACED as she waited for the two people outside the room to reach a decision.

Para ayudarme o no para ayudarme? To help me or not to help me?

She'd brought money to pay, though she didn't know the cost of a bodyguard service. She sank into a chair and put her head in her hands, fatigue from days on the run threatening to overcome her.

Her mind drifted back to six years ago, when she'd last met with

Jackson in a different, strange office. She'd been tired, terrified, alone, and desperate to keep her and her son safe.

She'd been twenty when she'd sat on a couch in the DEA's office, numb and utterly crushed in mind, body, and spirit. The fabric covering the stiff sofa had been abrasive and the overhead light unforgivingly bright.

Her father was dead. Her uncle would come after her.

She'd lost everything.

Not everything. She ran a hand through her son's hair as he slept on the cushions beside her. At almost two, he was a curled small ball. Innocent. Vulnerable.

But how could she protect the one person who mattered most to her?

The DEA wanted her statement as a witness to her father's murder. She was their key to chopping off the head of the cartel, and the DEA didn't care what the cost was to Daniela and her son. Their eyes held the truth they couldn't conceal. She was somebody's next pay raise, next promotion. A means to an end.

The minute she provided her statement, a target would be painted on her back. Maybe she was young, but she knew their demands wouldn't stop at a statement. They would want her to testify, and her uncle had men who could ensure she didn't survive that long.

And if the cartel used her son to get to her...

She shuddered.

Her other option was to throw herself at the mercy of her uncle and pledge loyalty to him. She would have to keep silent on the details of the murder of her father and hope Hermes let her and her son live.

She hadn't decided who would be the lesser of two evils—trust the US government to protect her or trust the cartel and the only family she'd ever known. Either option had her living—possibly not for very long—in constant fear.

The agent assigned to the case had left an hour ago, exasperated. Agent Rita Jones, whom Daniela recognized from two years ago as the woman who'd been fawning over her second cousin at her father's party, seemed hungry for Daniela's information. Too eager to be trusted. Too quick to make threats when Daniela refused to be pushed to sign binding documents. She was greedy for her own success without considering Daniela's perspective.

"Think of your son," Rita had implored.

Of course, Daniela was thinking of him.

"Do it for justice," Rita had demanded.

Whose justice?

Daniela's drug-selling uncle murdered her drug-selling father. Perhaps the biggest tragedy was how she and her father had finally been connecting. The birth of his first grandson had changed him. Suddenly, he became the doting father she'd always wanted. The type of father he'd once thought was a show of weakness.

And wasn't it just like a cartel lion to pounce when someone showed what was considered to be a weakness—affection?

Daniela had lost track of time at the DEA office, when the door opened and another suit entered—tall, blonde, and... her heart stopped. Jackson.

"Hello, Daniela." He gave her a soft, compassionate smile with a slightly apologetic air.

How many lonely nights had she fantasized about that smile? Jackson, who was clearly not an escort, sat down in the chair opposite her. She tried to process his real identity. So, this was what they truly were—opposites. A government agent and the daughter of a drug cartel leader.

But she couldn't hate Jackson for lying. In fact, she liked the idea that he was a man with a badge and a suit uniform rather than an escort. And, despite the one-night stand, which she'd accepted up front for what it would be, she'd always felt like that night with him had been a gift.

His words and actions made her feel more valuable in one night than anyone had in her entire life. She'd carried that self-worth every day since.

"DEA?" she asked.

"FBI. I was helping DEA Agent Jones with her undercover assignment the night you and I met." He kept his tone delicate, as though he expected her to lash out at him at any moment and was prepared to accept it.

Because he'd never exploited her vulnerability for knowledge, when he clearly served a badge, she couldn't be mad at him. Mostly, she could only envision how he'd looked naked and exposed—lean, pale body and sinewy muscles. The memory of his hands on her skin made her shiver.

She lowered her voice, although they were the only ones in the room besides Oscar. "Does the DEA or the FBI know about that night?"

Jackson shifted his weight. "They know we had a connection and talked for quite a while."

"That's what you put in your report?"

"Yes. That's why they called me in tonight."

Beside her, Oscar stirred.

"Is Jackson your real name?"

He nodded. "Jackson Hart." He glanced at the sleeping boy. "They didn't mention you had a son when they called me in to help. How old is he?"

"Twenty-one months." She watched the gears turn in Jackson's mind.

"Who's the father?"

"Not you."

"Okay."

"He's gone."

"Okay."

Silence settled for a beat as he stared at her son, but the boy faced the other way. Her stomach churned. The lie cost her something, but the truth would have cost her more.

"Can I get you something? Tea, sandwich?" he asked.

"They sent you to convince me to give a statement and testify."

"Yes. They want to put your uncle away for murder. After that, the two most prominent leaders of the cartel are eliminated." He winced at his own words, as if realizing he'd just referred to her father as 'eliminated.'

So thoughtful. So unlike other men in my life.

Glancing at his left hand, she noted he wore no wedding ring. Didn't matter. They'd shared a fleeting few hours together, nothing more would happen.

She swallowed. There would always be another leader to rise to the position. Not to mention that putting her uncle in jail didn't alleviate the danger she faced.

"I'm sorry about your father," Jackson said, sounding sincere.

"Even knowing what he was?"

"I'm sorry for you. Losing a father is a loss, no matter what crimes he's committed."

And she knew, right then, that she'd do whatever Jackson asked her to do. The authorities had played their ace in the hole. They had her where they wanted her. She didn't trust the US government, but she trusted Jackson. He'd lied about who he was to protect himself and Rita, but she was lying about her son to protect both of them. Despite his lie about his job, he'd given her a wonderful night without any other deception.

"If I agree to testify, then what?"

"Witness protection."

Yes. Agent Rita Jones had said as much.

"I become someone else for the rest of my life?"

"From this moment forward, you will already be someone else. You decide who that someone else is and how she best protects the people she loves."

People. Plural.

She had to protect her son, but now knowing who and what Jackson was, she would choose to protect him as well.

6

---

*D*aniela's head snapped up when Jackson and Mica returned to the conference room.

Jackson was tall like she remembered, but gone was any semblance of boyishness he'd still had at twenty-five when they'd first met. At thirty-three, his jaw looked firmer, his eyes sharper. Was his build beneath that suit the firm muscle she'd touched once—twice—before?

His blue eyes held resolution but a hint of sadness and reservation.

He knows Justin is his.

She'd wanted to be the one to tell him but hadn't stipulated that to Mica. Would he hate her for keeping him from him? Her stomach knotted. She would need to tell Justin at some point, but how could she? She had ripped her son from his old life. She didn't want to introduce his father without knowing how brief their time together might be.

Mica said, "It seems we're all in agreement to help you, Daniela. While we devise a plan, we need to keep you and Justin safe."

"They can stay at my place," Jackson offered. "The cartel doesn't know our history."

Daniela smiled at him, recalling when he'd said he had become an FBI agent to help people. Even now, in private security, he was eager to help. She hated she was putting him in danger, though.

Mica held up a hand to Jackson with the patience of a mother imploring her son not to jump ahead. "But WITSEC does, even if it's just a one-liner in someone's case file. If Daniela's concerns about someone in a position of authority outing her are true, then we need to assume they would know you two have a history. We need to assume Jackson will be on the list of people to look into, including his current employment."

Jackson's brow knit, and Daniela had the strange urge to kiss away his worry. She wasn't twenty anymore, and she knew nothing of the man Jackson had become. From what little she'd learned when she checked on him through an internet search once a year, he'd left the FBI and divorced his wife of four years around that time. Who was he now, and should Daniela tell him she still had feelings for him after all these years, when all they'd ever shared were two glorious nights?

"When are you next supposed to check in with WITSEC?" Mica asked.

"There is no check in. US authorities got what they wanted from me. My life or death now makes no difference to them." She couldn't keep the bitterness out of her tone.

"She's right," Jackson said. "WITSEC doesn't monitor or guard enrollees past the completed trial. Daniela is free to stay or leave. It's not meant to be neglectful. They can only do so much. However, they need to investigate how Daniela's identity was compromised, so we eventually need to let them know she was outed by someone."

Daniela doubted the US Marshals would believe her. They would think she'd jeopardized her identity, not them.

Mica rubbed a hand over her chin, brow furrowed in thought. "Since WITSEC doesn't know where you are, let's stow you at Jackson's place for only a few days. We'll add Rafe to the security detail. I need a couple of days to figure out where you can safely stay longer term."

"The cabin," Jackson suggested.

Mica shook her head. "I've avoided using it since it was compromised by the Shoup Group." She turned back to Daniela. "Get some rest today and tonight. Tomorrow, we'll discuss a plan."

Some of the pressure weighing on Daniela's chest these last several days eased. She took a deep breath, feeling a measure of hope for the first time since running from Sebastian.

"Thank you. Thank you both." Daniela clasped her hands together and nodded.

JACKSON DROVE his Dodge Ram while Daniela sat beside him and Justin sat in the back passenger seat. Mother and son both stared out the window. Mica was back at HQ making plans to hide Daniela's car in her father's mechanic's garage so it couldn't be used to trace Daniela to Atlanta. She was probably also brainstorming the next steps to help protect Daniela and her son.

His son.

Jackson fiddled with the air conditioning settings, feeling hot and confined in the vehicle despite its roominess. He had so many questions for Daniela, none of which he could ask in front of their child.

"What do you like to do for fun?" Jackson asked, glancing back at the boy.

"We had a neighborhood playground I liked. I had friends." Justin's sad tone tugged at Jackson's heart.

He suspected Justin had been told he'd never see them again. Because their identity had been uncovered, they could never return there or use those aliases again.

"It's tough losing friends," Jackson said. "We moved a lot when I was a boy because of my dad's work. Just when I was starting to belong, whoop, time to move again."

Justin asked, "What did you do about it?"

"The only thing I could do, I guess. I got great at meeting new people and making friends quickly."

"When am I going back to school?"

Daniela reached back and patted his knee. "We'll figure that out. I hope in a week or two. You won't get too far behind the other kids."

"What are we going to do all day at our new place?" Justin asked.

"There's a park in my neighborhood," Jackson offered.

Justin frowned.

"There isn't much at my house, but we won't be there but a few days. Maybe the next place will have more amenities." Jackson didn't entertain children and wondered if he had anything unsafe in his house. His gun would either be on him or unloaded. The only hazards he could think of applied to younger children—stairs, exposed outlets, and coffee table corners.

"Can I learn to shoot?" Justin asked.

Silence settled in the vehicle.

Your eight-year-old son is on the run from the Colombian cartel and asks if he can learn to shoot a deadly weapon. Now what?

Justin pressed, "Everyone is carrying a gun, including my mom. I want to learn to shoot."

"One day," Jackson began, glancing at Daniela, "if your mom approves, I'll take you to a gun range. For now, the last thing we want to do is to attract attention to ourselves."

"One day, Mom?"

"I can't think of anyone more qualified than Jackson to teach you self-defense," she said.

For the first time, Justin smiled, and Jackson's heart sputtered to see the similarity between them. How much of Justin's future was Daniela willing to let Jackson have a role in? He had so much to discuss with her but would wait until she was settled and they had a few moments alone.

I have a son. He hadn't been there for his birth or eight of his birthdays. Could he be there for future ones? Teach him to shoot? One day, teach him to shave and to drive?

Word of the day: kismet—fate, destiny. He hated what Daniela and Justin were going through, but perhaps kismet truly had brought them all together again.

Jackson slipped into silence, thinking back to the last time he'd seen Daniela and Justin.

AFTER A LONG DAY with US Marshals, he had parked his rental car in the driveway of the safe house. A motion sensor light had popped on, turning the darkness into a supernova.

Daniela sat still in the passenger seat while her young son slept in the car seat in the back. She was as beautiful as he remembered her at eighteen, despite a tired pair of eyes. As a mother at twenty, she was all young woman now—thinner cheeks and firmer mouth. Same impossibly long brown hair, though.

Jackson had yet to see the boy awake. He'd been asleep when he first saw Daniela at the DEA's office. After she agreed to testify and enter WITSEC, Jackson had been dismissed and the paperwork started. He was called back to take her to the safe house and watch over her until her US Marshal handler arrived the next morning. Apparently, Daniela had specifically requested him for the night duty, though he'd explained to her that he wouldn't know her new identity and wouldn't see her again after tomorrow. Before arriving to pick her up, he'd stopped and bought a car seat and a gift.

Daniela quietly exited the car and extricated her sleeping son from the back. He startled briefly before settling his head on her shoulders, eyes closed. Carrying the child, she followed Jackson in after he unlocked the door. She stayed in the entryway while he did a security sweep of the three-bedroom safe house.

"I'm going to tuck him into bed," she said.

"I'll unload the car." He closed the front door, walked to the car, and took out the single bag.

How devastated she must be to leave her old life behind and have nothing but a half-filled bag to take with her. Her WITSEC handler would get her set up with clothes and essentials, but life would never be the same for her.

Jackson brought the bag, as well as a gift wrapped in colorful balloon paper, into the house. When he heard the shower running in the other room, he searched the cabinets and found two cups and some chamomile tea.

By the time the tea was made and cooled to a drinking temperature, Daniela was out of the shower and joined him in the kitchen. She appeared to have found some spare clothes in the bedroom—baggy shorts and a T-shirt. Her head of damp hair had wet her shirt, making the thin fabric cling to her generous breasts.

The loose cotton partly obscured the curve of her waist, but he knew all the exquisite softness hidden from view. She was thinner but still with voluptuous hips and breasts enough to drive any man crazy. How many times had he fantasized about that night with her?

He shouldn't have slept with her—not only because he was an FBI agent but because she was seven years younger than him. She'd only been eighteen. He tried to console himself with how he'd made the experience about pleasure for her, but he'd still crossed lines that night. Lines that could have cost him his career, or his life, depending on who discovered the truth.

He offered her the cup of tea while leaning against the counter and sipping his own, grateful to occupy his hands with a task and keep them off her. He'd silently sworn to himself he wouldn't seduce her.

"Thank you." She sipped the beverage.

Her eyes looked as tired as her voice sounded, though they were still dark and alluring. Part of him wanted to gather her in his arms, hold her, and promise everything would work out. But she was off limits, and he couldn't make promises about events out of his control.

"What's this?" She gestured to the present on the kitchen table.

"For your son. It's magnetic building blocks." He shrugged uncomfortably. "It said for ages two and up, so I hope it's appropriate."

She smiled, but it didn't quite reach her eyes. "It's perfect. A new toy for a new beginning."

"At some point, it'll get easier, Daniela."

She set her tea down on the table and walked toward him, her jasmine scent wafting under his nose, reminding him of their first and only night together.

"I'll never see you again," she said.

"No." The sadness in his voice felt disproportionate to what paltry amount of time they'd ever spent together.

He placed his drink aside and reached back to grip the counter and keep his hands off her as he'd intended.

She took a step closer, a smokey seduction in her eyes, half covered by long lashes.

He swallowed and gripped the counter's edge more firmly, palms sweating now. "Daniela, we shouldn't—"

She raised a finger to his lips, silencing him. "The night we spent together was an incredible gift," she said. "I've never regretted it a day in my life. I hoped I might one day see you once more and tell you how amazing you made me feel. Now I have one last gift of seeing you again. Tomorrow you must leave. Forever. And it will be easier if you just leave. No goodbyes. Sneak out like an agent off to save the day and stop the bad guy. But tonight, you and I belong in the bedroom again. Maybe it wasn't the same fantastical night for you, but what matters to me is how I felt. How you made me feel. I want to feel that way again, even knowing it's only for tonight. And I think it will feel good for you, too."

During her speech, his hands had moved to rest on her hips. His heart thudded at their proximity and the heated look in her eyes. This woman was turning his world upside down all over again.

Even though he already knew what his answer would be, Jackson's mind took an extra second or two to weigh the pros and cons. He wanted Daniela and knew with absolute certainty that tonight would be even better than the last night they'd spent together. It saddened him to think this was all they would ever have, but they moved in vastly different spheres.

Sleeping with a witness could be catastrophic to his career, but Daniela had told no one about their first night together, and he trusted her not to tell anyone about tonight. He believed in her sincerity. Her actions in this moment weren't some sort of entrapment. His only regret tomorrow would be the end of what little time he'd been given to spend with her in this life.

He couldn't say no to this woman.

He pressed his fingers into the soft flesh on her hips, coaxing her body against his. "That night was amazing for me, too."

She rested her hands on his biceps and moved closer until her breasts pressed against his chest and her lips were mere millimeters away from his. When they kissed, she was smiling at first, reminding him of the first time he'd made her smile on the interior balcony of her father's house as they watched the party below. Like now, he'd known instantly he would do something recklessly wonderful, like sleep with her.

After a few tentative, tender moments, the kiss escalated with all the passion and fervor two people could cram into one last night together. She was practically climbing up him, deepening the kiss and raking hands through his hair. Unlike two years ago, there was no trace of hesitation or tentativeness on her behalf. Nothing was more flattering and arousing than this woman who couldn't get enough of him.

There were too many clothes between them, and they shed their garments on the way to the bedroom, where they embraced each other and tumbled into a night of ecstasy and fulfillment.

7

Daniela glanced at Jackson as he drove them to his house. He'd been quiet in thought as her nerves coiled with tension. She'd always wondered what she would say to this man if they ever met again. Now, her mind raced with ideas, but she couldn't say anything with Justin in the back seat. She also shouldn't trust herself on such little sleep after days of traveling on the run. Yes, a good night's sleep and then she could ask questions to learn who Jackson really was.

She wanted to know what he'd been up to all these years. What did he think about being a father? Why had he divorced? Why had he left the FBI?—though she was grateful he had. She wouldn't have run to a man with a badge, even if that man had been Jackson. She was already asking for impossible help from him. If he'd still been with the FBI, she would have been asking to ruin his career for her. Now, she was only asking him to risk his life.

She was putting her trust in a man she barely knew, but of all the things in life she couldn't trust, her heart was the exception. She could always trust the sensations of that ever-beating organ. It warmed when she held her son, fluttered for the man who'd given her that gift, and fiercely pumped the adrenaline she'd needed to flee from danger on more than one occasion.

Her heart trusted Jackson, and she had latched onto that in her darkest hours when she'd fled for her life. Now, he was willing to help—no questions, no stipulations. She needed to tread carefully so she didn't hurt him—physically or emotionally.

"Thank you for helping us," she said, breaking the silence.

"Of course. It means a lot to me that you came to me for help."

Oof. Her gut clenched. Yes, she needed to be careful not to damage Jackson emotionally. If danger escalated beyond what Rider SI could mitigate, she might need to disappear. If Jackson became too attached, she could hurt him.

If she had to disappear, would he go with her? Justin was his son, after all.

She was getting ahead of herself. They didn't know each other, and Jackson had a life and career here in Atlanta.

"When we get settled, I need to work for a few minutes," she said.

"Oh?"

"I do freelance ghostwriting and insurance claims. Quite different, I know. Both are all online, so I can work anywhere, but I don't want to suffer critical reviews by delivering work late. I have a few projects to complete. These jobs need to be here for me when this is over."

"You can work. You have a laptop or do you need to use my computer?"

"Laptop."

"Okay. I remember you wanted to be a nurse."

"I told several people from my old life about that ambition for nursing school. WITSEC said I couldn't be anyone I was or anyone I had verbalized wanting to be."

"I'm sorry."

"This work suits me better. Turns out, sometimes I nearly faint at the sight of blood."

Justin chuckled. "Yeah. I got a bloody nose on the playground one time, and she had to sit down and put her head between her knees."

Daniela turned and patted his knee. She puffed out her lips in a part frown, part pout. "*Gracias por eso*, blabbermouth. You're supposed to tell other people how invincible and amazing your mother is."

"Your secret's safe with me." Jackson smiled. "Before you use your laptop, let's connect with Claire and make sure there's nothing planted on it that can trace you. Then, you can work in my home office. Maybe Justin and I can toss a football in the backyard for a little exercise."

Could her computer have been tracked? She hadn't considered that and had used it a few times on her trip. She rubbed her temple a moment. "Yes, please check it."

WHEN JACKSON PARKED in his driveway, Rafe stood on his porch and waved. He wore jeans and a button-down shirt, with his long hair pulled back in a ponytail. He had bronze skin from his South American heritage. The man smiled infrequently, and with the jagged scar trailing down one side of his face, he could look intimidating.

Mica had said she would add Rafe to the protection detail. She must have texted him at some point after the conference room meeting. Jackson was glad to have his trusted partner working on this one.

"I'll introduce you to my partner, Rafe," he told Daniela as he turned off the truck engine.

The sun was lowering against a pale blue sky as Jackson, Daniela, and Justin each grabbed a bag and walked from the driveway along the path to the front door. The early fall night held both the promise of cool days to come and the memory of humid days past. Jackson's subdivision had a hundred homes with curving streets, sidewalks, and cul du sacs. He liked the quiet neighborhood in Roswell, though the lots were small and the houses packed close. His two-story home had simple gables and a brick and siding facade.

Daniela led, followed by Justin, then Jackson. Jackson opened his mouth to warn mother and son, when Justin slipped on the slick walkway.

Jackson dropped his bag and caught the boy before he landed on his backside. "Whoop. There you go," he said as he righted him. "Sorry about that. This stretch is always slippery after the sprinklers run. I don't know why the previous owners laid flagstone down with no anti-slip coating. It's on my list of house repairs."

They piled near the front door, where Jackson withdrew keys. "Rafe, this is Daniela and her son Justin."

My son. The thought made his head spin again.

Rafe took Daniela's bag and shook her hand. "Pleasure." He turned to Justin. "Nice to meet you."

"Thank you for being on the team," Daniela said.

"*De nada,*" Rafe gave a slight bow of his head.

Jackson unlocked the door, stepped inside, and walked to his alarm pad. Entering the code, he disabled the alarm, only to reactivate it when everyone had entered.

"The alarm needs to be deactivated to go in or out," he said. "I'm not giving either of you the code because you don't exit without an escort unless it's an emergency—a fire or intruder inside the house. Exits are the front and back doors and all windows, preferably on the first floor, but there is a fire ladder coiled in the upstairs hall linen closet that can be used if needed."

He showed them around, then, while they settled, he made sandwiches. They ate ham and Swiss on rye in relative silence. He didn't push for conversation because mother and son both looked exhausted.

While they ate, Rafe got on the phone with Claire and had her walk him through a sweep of Daniela's computer.

"No signs of tampering," he reported, nodding at Jackson and sliding the laptop back toward Daniela.

After sandwiches, she slipped away to work, while Jackson took Justin into his small backyard to throw a football. The day was fading to gray, but enough light lingered for them to toss the ball.

"What questions do you have for me, Justin? I'm sure this must be a scary few days." Jackson tossed the ball easily because he didn't know if the boy had ever thrown a football.

His own son.

He didn't know when or if Daniela would make that world-colliding announcement to Justin, but Jackson felt this was her decision and should possibly be wedged between some serious therapy sessions.

His son caught the ball and threw it back. *Decent form*, Jackson thought, feeling a brief pang. His son's first time throwing a football hadn't been with his father.

"I'm worried about Mom," Justin said. "She tries to hide it, but she's scared."

"We're going to help her. Both of you." Jackson tossed the ball with a little more force.

Justin caught it with ease. "Your company. You protect people?"

"That's right."

"How many people work there?"

"Rider SI has a dozen employees. We're deployed all over the world with high-profile clients and everyday folk."

"You ever saved anyone's life?"

"I'd tell you, but then I'd have to..."

Justin grinned.

"Kidding," Jackson said.

Justin giggled, and Jackson instantly knew he would work to bring the boy all the happiness he could to elicit more of those laughs.

"I can tell you instances, just not names. Yes, I've saved lives." Now wasn't the time for modesty. The boy needed to know Jackson and the Rider team were capable.

The football continued spinning through the air, back and forth.

"I took down a helicopter with an Explorer," Jackson added.

"Really?" Justin's eyebrows lifted to his hairline. "Was it filled with enemy goons?"

Jackson laughed. "Yeah, it had a few enemy goons. They were attacking a family my team and I were assigned to protect."

"Is the family okay?"

"Alive and well to this day."

"The family had children? You've protected kids before?"

Jackson caught the ball. Rolling it in his hands, he felt the textured surface and looked at the white seam. When he raised his eyes to Justin, he said, "With my life."

SEBASTIAN TOOK a drag off his Pall Mall. He had traveled from visiting his father in California to his estate in Cuernavaca. He loved this slice of paradise in the Land of Eternal Spring. The high stone walls topped in shards of glass and surrounding cameras leant safety, though they sometimes made him wonder if he wasn't in prison as well. A gilded cage, of sorts. Though, sitting out by the pool as the sun shone let him forget his troubles, albeit temporarily.

A cardinal, bright red against a sky of blue, streaked past his view and into a nearby jacaranda tree, and his mind drifted to Robert Frost's *Acceptance*.

> *When the spent sun throws up its rays on cloud*
> *And goes down burning into the gulf below,*
> *No voice in nature is heard to cry aloud*
> *At what has happened.*
> *Birds, at least must know.*

Find Daniela, his father's command invaded Sebastian's thoughts.

She'd looked good when he'd glimpsed her through the car window. Tall and slender but still had generous curves where it counted. Her sad eyes hadn't changed. He'd bet they could still turn to fire in a fight. How much alike were they? Their fates had been decided by who their parents were.

Where would you run to, little Daniela?

'*A woman always runs to a man.*'

His father made such insulting and sweeping generalities. But sometimes they were true.

A man.

When had Sebastian ever seen her with a man? Visions of younger Daniela flashed through Sebastian's mind. At sixteen, one of his friends had made a pass at her, but nothing came of it. She'd obviously slept with someone to have had Oscar, but when Sebastian had asked her about the father years ago, she'd told him she'd forced him to run away so as not to face Alejandro's wrath. Sebastian hadn't thought to ask the man's name when she seemed reluctant to talk about it.

A different man came to Sebastian's mind. Nine years ago, at one of her father's parties at his California estate, Daniela had sat near the banister, overlooking the party as she often did. Sebastian had stood in the corner, watching the party as well. The scent of drugs, sex, and alcohol floated on the air and mixed with the music.

A man had sat next to her, and they appeared to have a conversation. The image stuck in Sebastian's mind because Daniela looked happy talking to him, and the man wasn't someone Sebastian knew. He'd also thought the situation seemed odd because the tall, handsome American had arrived with a date, but that woman had been crawling over Juan like a cat in heat.

"Diego, do you remember Alejandro César's party at his La Jolla estate years ago when I would have been about eighteen?" Sebastian flicked his ash away as he adjusted in his lounge chair.

"Vaguely." The man set down the phone he'd been quietly thumbing. "Oh, yeah, that was the night Leo got wasted and swam naked in the pool."

"Juan bedded a woman that night."

"Guava or Estrella?"

"Juan Guava."

Diego's lips curved in a creepy smile. "I'm sure he did."

"The woman he slept with arrived with a man. The man spent the evening talking to Daniela."

"You want to track down a man Daniela talked to almost a decade ago at one of your uncle's parties? If we track down every man a woman ever talked to, we'll take a year to find your cousin using that approach." Diego resumed texting—or playing Candy Crush, or whatever the brute did to entertain his simple, uncultured mind.

Sebastian took another drag off his cigarette. Unlikely to work, he agreed, but Diego didn't know Daniela the way Sebastian did. Men overlooked her. When he'd known her, he'd seen boys and men spend their affections on thinner, flimsier women with thinner, flimsier minds. Not the daughter of the cartel if they valued their life. This man, however, had taken the time to sit beside her at a party and strike up a conversation. Sebastian hadn't seen them again that night. His vague recollection didn't mean a connection had formed, but the memory was a place to start.

The odds were next to nothing that the gringo was a viable lead, but what the hell did Sebastian have to do but chase useless leads in the never-ending fruitless pursuit of his father's appreciation?

"You've something better to do? Or a better idea?" Sebastian asked Diego, a hard edge to his voice that sounded eerily akin to his father's. Sebastian hated it, but the tone served its purpose.

Diego looked over at him, clearly hearing the directive in Sebastian's tone. "No."

"Okay." Sebastian shoved off the lounge chair, tugging his green silk robe around him. "Let's talk to Juan. See if he remembers the woman with the *gringo*."

8

———————

$\mathcal{J}$ackson woke at five a.m. and stepped outside for some refreshing activity. Wisps of moisture curled out of his mouth when he exhaled, and the cool air felt invigorating. In a few weeks, the leaves would change colors, and a drive through north Georgia would reveal a beautiful spread of yellows, oranges, and reds over the mountainsides.

He itched to do his usual morning run through his neighborhood but wouldn't dare leave Daniela and Justin alone. Rafe had stayed until after dinner last night and wasn't due back over for another hour. Jackson had opted for a round of pushups, squats, and sit-ups to burn off some of his restless energy.

He'd wanted to talk to Daniela last night, but she'd been so exhausted after tucking Justin into bed that Jackson had let her retire to his spare room. She'd briefly mentioned wanting to meet with the cartel before giving him a thank you and disappearing behind a closed door.

Meet with the cartel. With that bit of terrifying information, he'd sent a text to one of his FBI friends before retiring to his own room, where he'd barely slept, mind still reeling with Daniela's arrival back in his life and the new knowledge of his son.

After wiping his brow, Jackson slung the towel over his shoulder and stepped back through his back sliding glass door. The coffee he'd started before his work-out routine was finished brewing, and he poured a cup, followed by a splash of cream.

He felt Daniela's presence before he even turned around.

"Coffee. *Mi héroe.*"

He plucked a mug from the cupboard and handed it to her, paying attention to how much she poured and how much cream she added. Her dark hair, which came to one third down her back, was braided. He remembered the locks being down to her waist and wondered if she'd cut it short when she initially went into WITSEC only to let it grow over the last six years. She was wearing the t-shirt he'd given her last night to sleep in and her jeans from yesterday. He made a mental note to take her and Justin clothes shopping.

"I have sugar," he offered.

"I'm sweet enough." Her lips curved.

That you are, precious Daniela.

A smiling Daniela in his house wearing his t-shirt. This was a fantasy come true... minus the cartel hunting her.

"I agree with that. Did you sleep okay?" he asked.

"Yes. Soundly, knowing we had a bodyguard under the same roof. I haven't felt safe for days." She wrapped her hands around her mug and slid onto the stool by his counter.

"I'm glad you came to me." He sipped his coffee.

"Me too. I was worried. I lied to you the last time we saw each other. Yesterday, I was afraid you'd be angry when you learned about Justin." She sipped her coffee.

He shook his head. "Hurt, not angry. I'm sad to think I missed the first eight years of his life, but you were in an impossible predicament. I understand why you didn't tell me."

"I'm sorry for having to keep your son a secret from you." She locked eyes with him.

He swallowed, not liking the anguish and turmoil in her tone. She'd probably faced enough of those two emotions in her life without this secret. Keeping that information from him must have hurt her, too. He wouldn't be angry with her over this and add to her hardship.

"Justin is a good name. Strong." He sipped his coffee.

Daniela smiled wistfully. "My father named him Oscar. I didn't have a choice in the matter, because I had disgraced Alejandro by conceiving in sin." She said the words lightly, as though she didn't share her father's religious sentiments and felt no shame in having a child. "But it was a fun name. Naming his grandson was the start of his blossoming affection for his new family... after his initial outrage, of course. When I went into WITSEC, they let me pick a new name. Justin means just. I named him for you, Jackson. A man who went into law enforcement. A man after justice. A just man."

A lump formed in his throat. "I'm not in law enforcement anymore." Part of him worried she had put him on a pedestal all these years. What if he couldn't live up to the expectations she'd created around a mythical lawman?

"Ah, but you are in a different form of justice now. Actually, I like this one better. You help people who hire you because you want to help. Not because some keyboard-typing office worker gave you an assignment." She swirled her coffee before taking another sip.

"I lost my badge, Daniela. Resigned it."

"You wear the badge of honor, not some document printed on a piece of paper by a government entity."

"When—"

A knock at the door interrupted their conversation.

"Rafe, reporting for duty," said the voice from outside.

"To be continued." Jackson walked past Daniela and gave her shoulder a squeeze.

He disarmed the alarm, let Rafe in, and reset it.

"Ah, I smell coffee." Rafe wore jeans and a grey t-shirt, hair back in its usual ponytail.

"Kitchen. Help yourself." Jackson told him.

"Daniela," Rafe waved at her as he meandered into the kitchen.

"Hi, Rafe. I'm going to focus on my computer and get a little work done before Mica arrives." She disappeared into her room.

"She holding up, okay?" Rafe asked, pouring a cup of coffee. He turned to the freezer, plucked an ice cube, and added it to his beverage. Apparently, he needed the caffeine boost now and didn't want to wait for it to cool.

"I think so. Let's talk outside." Jackson motioned for Rafe to follow.

They went to the front porch, where Jackson dusted off the cushioned wicker chairs and they sat.

Jackson leaned back. "I'll be honest. I'm reeling a bit."

"Mica told me the boy is yours. Surprise! You have a family. That would shock anyone. Even worse to find out they're in danger."

"Word of the day: moonstruck. Unable to think or act normal, especially because of love."

Rafe blinked. "You love this woman you barely know?"

Jackson held up a finger. "Moonstruck. I didn't say love. Every time I see her, it's like an arrow straight to the heart. And this is only my third time seeing her."

Beautiful, resilient Daniela. She was back in his life like an apparition, but this time, part of him wanted to grab on and never let go. "I have this urge to ground her and give her the home and safety she's never had, but my two brief encounters with her don't mean I know her."

Jackson had made a mistake in his last relationship of thinking if you love someone, life would all work out. If you love each other, you'd want the same things—home life, family, future. Reality had slowly crushed his naivety. He still hadn't been willing to let go until the adultery. He'd drawn the line somewhere.

Rafe shrugged, taking a sip of his coffee. "You have time to learn more about Daniela while protecting her. You can see if this moonstruck is love or lust."

Lust was certainly part of the equation based on the way Jackson's hormones flashed images of his past encounters with the woman. Daniela only had to walk past him to seduce him into giving in to physical temptation. But while a tumble under the sheets might distract her from her current unfortunate situation, sex wasn't how he would discover more about the woman she'd become and the future she hoped to build when this was over.

Jackson shifted his weight in the chair. "I'd like to find out if there's a future between us." He would learn about Daniela's hopes and dreams before he pushed his way into a relationship with her. He scrubbed a hand over his face. "She's been in hiding so long, she might not even know what she wants in her future." Maybe they could find out together while he fulfilled his urge to keep her safe.

"Rafe, I have a son. A son!" Jackson smiled and punched Rafe in the arm.

Rafe rubbed his arm. "I feel like we need a cigar for this part of the conversation."

"I want to be a part of Justin's life, and not just for this brief interlude of the mission." His enthusiasm deflated as he leaned back in the chair again. "But he doesn't know."

"Are you going to tell him?"

Jackson sipped his coffee. "I feel like that information should come from his mother. First, she'll need to trust me."

"She came to you for help. That's trust."

"Trust or desperation?" Jackson countered. "Daniela has never been given a reason to trust anyone, including me."

Both of their encounters had ended with them sleeping together. But sex didn't automatically equate with trust. Their long conversation during the party had been lovely and led to a night of passion he hadn't expected or orchestrated. But that wasn't necessarily how such a thing might be viewed by an eighteen-year-old with years of solitude in which to reflect. Or by an outsider looking in.

The second time had been orchestrated, but by her. Once again, his actions might look like that of an opportunist preying on a woman in crisis, but at the time, he'd felt like he was pulling a drowning woman out of the water and offering a warm blanket of comfort, however temporary.

Maybe he'd been fooling himself. Maybe he had taken advantage of her, and if that was true, he would have to show her their nights together had meant something to him.

Had they meant something to her?

Jackson sighed, recognizing Rafe was quietly waiting for more.

He leaned forward, elbows on his knees, gripping his mug with two hands. "I have two leading theories for why she came to me. First, after our brief interactions, she truly trusts me and understands that in our time together I was trying to give her something—give us both something—in a lonely, cruel world. The second possibility is that she doesn't trust me, but she's taking a chance that a man would fulfill his biological drive to protect his offspring and the woman who bore him."

"Only one way to find out," Rafe said. "You need to ask her."

MICA DROVE to Jackson's house. Now that everyone had a night's rest, they needed to talk strategy. The sane strategy was tucking Daniela and Justin back under the wing of WITSEC, but Mica understood the woman's reluctance. Someone had leaked Daniela's location. She would never feel safe under US Marshal protection again. Mica had Claire looking into possible leaks, but discovering the traitor didn't translate into another six years of safety for Daniela.

Mica wound through Jackson's neighborhood and parked behind his truck in the driveway. He was one of her newer employees, and she hadn't been to his house before now. The quaint neighborhood looked ideal for Jackson's new-found family, but she worried about how events would play out.

Judging by how quickly Jackson had leapt to his family's aid—and Mica admired him for it—he might not stay with Rider SI if it meant leaving them. If Daniela and Justin went back into WITSEC, Mica suspected Jackson would follow. If mother and son needed to disappear to another country across the globe, Jackson would likely migrate with them. And if that happened, Mica might lose a valuable employee.

Jackson greeted her at the door and led her inside his home. She sat in his living room on a cushioned chair while Jackson and

Daniela perched on the sofa. Cups of half consumed coffee rested on the low table in front of them. They didn't sit close like an intimate couple, but by the way Jackson looked at Daniela, Mica suspected a relationship was only a matter of time.

"Rafe is throwing the ball with Justin in the backyard," Jackson said.

Mica nodded, acknowledging Jackson letting her know they were free to converse.

"I want a meeting with the cartel," Daniela said.

"You want to meet with Hermes César? The man who wants to kill you?" Mica's mind churned, thinking about the logistics as she infused her voice with incredulity. They could probably get Daniela safely in and out of the prison visitation center. Of course, that would create a trail, and Mica wasn't ready to let the cartel know Daniela was under Rider protection.

"I want to meet with whoever my uncle is giving orders to. Whoever is second in command while Hermes is in prison."

"Why?"

"Maybe I can reason with him. The cartel is a billion-dollar industry. A lucrative business. Why waste time and resources on a revenge scheme? I'm an ant to their empire. The small nip I inflicted by testifying was over six years ago. The damage is done to both our lives." She paused, then held up a finger. "Or maybe those men were just sent to scare me. I'd like to know if my uncle truly intends to kill me after all these years."

Mica pursed her lips. "If I understand correctly, you want to meet with the cartel leader's second in command. This meeting would determine if they intend to harm you, and if so, provide you the opportunity to talk them out of it." Before Daniela could interrupt, Mica mimicked her with a raised finger. "All the while, my team is supposed to prevent them from killing you on sight."

Daniela rubbed her hands together. "We will agree on a safe location. I don't want to put anyone on your team in danger."

Mica rubbed her temples. Daniela was correct in that, at this point, they didn't even know if she and Justin were targets. The intention behind the scare at Daniela's home wasn't clear. Had it been a sloppy surveillance job or a sloppy hit? A meeting might help Mica discover the magnitude of the threat, but at tremendous risk.

However, Daniela's plan might also help Mica keep Jackson aboard Rider SI. If there was no threat to his family, perhaps they could remain out of hiding and stay with him.

"Jackson asked for my team to help you," Mica said. "I don't commit to half-baked plans. If I agree to this—which I'm not saying I am—we need a safe location with no weapons. Like an airport terminal where everyone goes through security first."

Neutral territory. Mica had her office building equipped with a weapon detector in the elevator, but that was a warning system, not a prevention mechanism. She also wouldn't want to meet them in Atlanta and give away Daniela's location.

Daniela's gaze turned contemplative as she picked up her mug and took a slow sip of coffee. "A church. We can meet at a church. They won't attack on sacred ground."

Mica cocked her head to one side. "Um. They're drug dealers, not vampires."

"They're Catholics."

Mica pursed her lips. "I'm sure *The Holy Bible* doesn't say you can kill anywhere except in a church. You're putting a lot of faith in their religious disposition to congregate with an enemy under a cross."

"They won't instigate a fight in the church," Daniela said with absolute conviction. "Now, entering and exiting the church is fair game, so we need to be prepared for an attack before or after the meeting."

"Jackson?" Mica turned to stare at him. "Your thoughts?"

He placed a hand on Daniela's shoulder. "I'm backing Daniela. If we can find a way to meet safely, we can better assess the threat. Bonus points if they can also see she's not alone and defenseless."

Mica would need to brainstorm a plan with several contingencies and pull some team members for a couple of days to help.

Safely, being the operative word, Mica thought.

9

─────────

After Mica left, Daniela and Justin curled up together in front of the television and watched *The Mandalorian*.

Jackson stepped outside onto his back porch. Across the fence, one of his neighbors pulled weeds in her backyard, but she was out of earshot. Jackson called his FBI contact and former colleague Special Agent Eddie Finch.

"Jackson, you texted me twelve hours ago. How about a little more patience?" Eddie wasn't known for his winning personality, but he helped friends in need.

"I'll listen to whatever you know so far."

Eddie sighed. "The César cartel is the largest Colombian organized crime syndicate. One of the largest in South America. Drugs mostly, but they also engage in tourist kidnappings for ransom, sex trafficking, and extortion. What mess is Rider in now that they're tangling with a Colombian cartel?"

Jackson ignored Eddie's dig and asked, "Who's the acting leader with Hermes in prison?"

"His son, Sebastian César."

"Is he wanted for anything on US soil?" Jackson wondered if he could lure him here and get him arrested. Of course, that probably would do nothing to keep Daniela safe. Prison didn't seem to stop men of power from enacting their will.

"No, he's clean. He has an army of men to do his illegal deeds."

"Okay. Thanks for the help. Anything you can share with me about the cartel would be helpful."

Another sigh. "Does this have something to do with the rumors about you and Alejandro César's daughter from years ago?"

"Eddie, you know how this works. The less you know, the better." Jackson trusted Eddie, but he wouldn't share any details about Daniela. As far as Eddie knew, Daniela was someone else in WITSEC still.

"Fine. Don't get into the habit of coming to me for information. I'm helping you as a friend, but I don't support the Rider team and their blurred lines of upholding the law." Eddie had always been a stickler for following the law to the letter, but Jackson suspected his friend had some level of grudging respect for Rider SI, because he had been the one to connect Jackson and Mica when Jackson was leaving the FBI.

"Understood. And appreciated." Jackson disconnected the call as he paced his backyard.

Next, he called Claire. "Good morning. How are you today, Claire?"

"Uh, huh. Whilst I appreciate your congeniality, I know you're at like DEFCON five emotionally right now. Cut to the chase and tell me what you need."

"You're amazing."

"So I'm told," she said sweetly.

"I need a phone number for Sebastian César, acting leader of the César cartel."

Clicking keys sounded in the background. "A number? We're just calling up drug dealers directly these days?"

"Seems so," he said, walking to his grill and dusting off leaves and pine pollen on top.

"Why isn't Mica making the call?" Claire asked.

"Machismo. She thought a male drug cartel leader would take

another man more seriously." He lifted the lid, inspected the inside, and noted he would need to clean out old ash from the grill.

"Ugh. Well, that's just... probably accurate." She scoffed. "Okay. I have a few options. He has a home in Colombia. Anapoima to be more specific. Vacation estate in Cuernavaca. Mobile phone."

"Can you send them all to me? Also, I need a church."

"You and Mica both, so I'm guessing you're wanting the same—Catholic, not in the state of Georgia, and somewhere I can get a direct flight out of Hartsfield."

"Yes. And with an escape route not readily apparent from the exterior or from standard internet sources." He paced his porch.

"Working on it."

"Thanks, Claire. You're one in a million."

"Then stick around, will you? Mica's all worried you're going to run off with Daniela." Keys continued to click.

"She is?" He stopped pacing. He didn't want to leave Rider SI. He loved his job and the family he'd formed with them. "That would be an absolute last resort."

"Let's make sure events don't digress in that direction," Claire said. "I've sent the numbers. And... now I've sent the church information."

"Thanks, Claire."

When he disconnected the call, he sent Mica a quick text. After a brief back-and-forth communication, they settled on a day and time of the meet, and Mica gave him the thumbs up emoji to make the call.

Jackson dialed Sebastian's mobile phone through an app that would block Sebastian from seeing his number.

"Sebastian." The voice held a Latino accent.

"Daniela wants a meet," Jackson said.

"Who is this?"

"Her bodyguard." Jackson let a few beats of silence pass before adding, "The day after tomorrow at Saint Patrick's Cathedral in Midtown Manhattan." He paced his back porch again.

"That's quite short notice. I will have to fly internationally." His voice was silky smooth, a too-relaxed purr under the circumstances.

"Resourceful man like yourself, I'm sure you'll manage."

"I expect to see Daniela there."

"You will."

"Then let me speak with her now and verify she's with you."

"She's with me, and she's safe."

"You're not a Marshal with WITSEC. They wouldn't do something like this," Sebastian said.

"Bodyguard, not US Marshal. Saint Patrick's Cathedral in Midtown Manhattan. Five o'clock." Jackson ended the call.

At the slide of his backdoor, he turned to watch Daniela step outside. Loose strands of hair from her braid waved in the breeze. He wanted to touch them, run the silky texture between his fingers. But they weren't on intimate terms where he could touch her at will.

"We have a meet," he told her, tucking his phone in his pocket and shoving his hands in them for good measure.

"Who is in charge?"

"Hermes' son."

Her shoulders sagged. "Oh, poor Sebastian. He was the one who found me, but I didn't consider he would actually be in a leadership role. When do we meet him?"

Poor Sebastian? Jackson wondered about her relationship with her cousin before she went into hiding. He would have to ask her sometime.

"Day after tomorrow," he said.

Her eyes widened. "So soon?"

He pulled his hands out of his pockets but resisted the urge to wrap her in his arms and offer the comfort he thought she needed. He didn't want to be intrusive. "Gives them less time to prepare."

"And us." She shivered.

He stepped toward her reflexively and rubbed his hands up and down her arms. So much for keeping his hands off her. "We'll be prepared."

When she leaned into him, he took the invitation and enveloped her in his arms. He wished he could keep her right here, always. Mica was right to be concerned. If he had to choose between continuing to work at Rider SI or whisking Daniela and Justin off to a new identity, he would choose mother and son.

EVENTS MOVED FASTER than Daniela had expected. Already, she was packed and soon to be headed to her meeting with the top cartel leader. Why did it have to be Sebastian? On the other hand, maybe she could appeal to the emotions of her once beloved cousin.

She'd passed yesterday planning and being amazed at the Rider Team's ability to pivot fast and take an offensive approach to a situation. They were so busy plotting and packing that Daniela had little time alone with Jackson. When he'd embraced her yesterday, she had wondered what falling asleep in his arms every night might feel like. So warm, so safe. She'd never simply slept in a man's embrace.

She'd been around him a short time and was already wanting more of the passion they'd once shared. What would he think if he knew she was forming an attachment so quickly and with so little wisdom on the matter?

Meanwhile, Jackson had miles of relationship experience beyond her. He'd been married. He must have spent long nights in the arms of a woman. But something failed between the two of them, and with no children to share. Each woman had a part of Jackson the other hadn't—one a marriage, the other a child.

Daniela climbed into Justin's bed to tuck him in for the night. She owed him an explanation about her upcoming departure. He gave her a tired smile as she brushed the hair off his forehead.

"The prince is going to meet with one of the king's delegates to talk about peace," she said.

"Will they hurt you?" Justin asked.

"No. No. We agreed to meet. That's all."

"In most movies, even *Star Wars*, 'diplomatic negotiations' ended in fighting."

She smiled despite the tension twisting in her gut that seemed to be her new companion since fleeing her home. "Just a brief meeting, then I'll be back home. You're going to stay with Mica. She's nice, right?" Daniela wanted to veer off the topic of the meeting with the mafia.

Justin shrugged.

"You'll have a good time. I want to hear an excellent report on manners."

"Okay."

"We'll talk every day while I'm gone."

"Okay."

She pulled him into her arms. "Survive this, we will."

He chuckled at her Yoda voice. Someday, he would find her antics annoying, but for now, he was in a fun phase of his youth where his mom was amusing and he still liked hugs.

MICA DROVE Justin to her house after Daniela had said goodbye to him. Jackson and Mica had assured Daniela that Justin would be safe with Mica while she made the trip with Jackson to New York. Daniela had held herself together remarkably well during the parting. She'd obviously never spent time away from her son, but she'd chosen to confront the cartel and couldn't take him into danger.

In the back seat, Justin was quiet.

"I know this is a lot to take in," Mica told him. "We'll have a laid back few days, and your mom will be back in no time."

"Yeah."

"Anything in particular you want for meals while you're with me?"

"No."

"For somebody with all As, you're awfully monosyllabic."

Justin grunted with a smirk that reminded Mica of Jackson.

"Ah, you know that word. You must have a good vocabulary."

"I won the school spelling bee."

"Oh, wow. Congratulations."

"Mom does ghostwriting, and sometimes she has me edit her work. She says I'm a good thesaurus."

"Your mom's a smart woman using you as a resource. What do you get paid for that?"

"She says I get a roof over my head and clothes on my back."

Ah, so she's a genius.

Mica chuckled. "That's a very mom thing to say."

"Yeah."

Mica's two-story house in the north Atlanta suburbs had a small lawn and fenced back yard. The red brick contrasted nicely with the charcoal shingles on the roof. When they pulled into her driveway, David walked out, carrying Allen.

"Speaking of moms," Mica said, "that's my son, Allen."

Justin's eyebrows raised in curiosity, and he exited the car without being prompted. As Mica walked around to grab his bag containing a change of clothes and toothbrush, David introduced himself. He had a warm smile and disarmingly disheveled brown hair.

"I'm David. This is Allen."

"Sup, little man?" Justin bumped his fist into the one Allen had hanging in the air.

The toddler's green gaze went doe-eyed, and Mica was certain Justin had just made a new best friend. At the very least, another small person would fascinate the toddler enough to follow him around for the next few days.

"How old is he?" Justin asked.

"Two and change."

"Seems cool."

"You should see him during temper tantrums." At Justin's puzzled look, she added, "There was the meltdown at a breakfast diner because I wouldn't let him lick his shoe. Or the time in the grocery store where I wouldn't open the strawberry jam so he could spoon it out and eat it. Not that he's ever been allowed to do that at home. Or the time we were at a friend's house, and I wouldn't let him eat the dog's food."

Justin chuckled. "Kids, right?" His tone suggested he didn't think he was part of that group, which made Mica laugh.

"Come on in," David said. Letting Justin lead, he turned back to Mica to give her a welcome home kiss. "Seems like a nice kid."

"Yeah, sorry to bring work home."

"You did the right thing."

"You got the stuff?" Mica asked.

"I did."

"Thanks."

Inside, shopping bags were strewn on the kitchen counter.

David set Allen down, who immediately walked to Justin.

David gestured to the bags. "Mica said you had little more than the clothes on your back, so she charged me with picking up a few basics. I found a few *Star Wars* t-shirts because I heard you're into the shows. There are pants and underwear and toiletries, too."

"Cool." Justin glanced in the bag, then down at Allen, who'd latched onto his leg. "You want to check this stuff out with me, little man?" After picking up the bags, he walked to the living room and sat on the floor where Allen could rummage through the bags with him.

"Don't worry. I'll pick the bags up off the floor when they're done," David told Mica.

"Thanks." Mica took her gun out of its holster and unloaded it.

David pulled the case from above the refrigerator, and Mica stored the gun inside before locking it and putting it back above the fridge. She was aware of Justin watching, even as he played with Allen on the floor. She wouldn't hide the fact that she carried a weapon. He was in danger and would have to mentally adjust to armed protection until that danger passed.

Last, she pulled out another gun, this one from her work bag. The weapon had a long, slender barrel.

"What's this?" David inspected it.

"Claire's been working on a tranquilizer gun. The late Peter Shoup—" Rider's last adversary in the dark security world "—had men carrying something like this. When they injected Rafe, he says he went lax pretty quick. I charged Claire with creating something similar. She worked with Bill Sharp's R&D team. Because Jenna and Jess work in the ICU, they helped with what concoction of sedatives to use."

"When do I get to be a paid consultant for cool new gadgets?" David placed the tranq gun above the fridge as well. As an ER physician, he would know sedatives also, but the man was already a full-time physician and full-time dad.

Mica grinned. "I can try it out on you? We need to test it on people before we use it in the field."

"That's a hard pass. Why are you carrying it around if you haven't tested it?"

She shrugged. "I have no moral issue with shooting a bad guy and seeing what happens."

David shook his head with an amused grin. "I'm going to get working on dinner."

"I'll get Justin settled in."

She began by making the bed in the guest room. She'd never had a client's child under her roof before now. Although Daniela wasn't even technically a client, because no way would Mica take Daniela's money—her son was one of Mica's employee's sons. Daniela and Justin felt more like Mica's work family than clients.

Rider SI had protected families, but this felt closer and more dangerous than her secure-and-deliver arrangements. This was uncharted territory, and she wasn't sure how they would navigate the hazardous cartel when they were after one of their own.

10

Outside the window, the wing of the plane cut through clouds. Jackson struggled with how to comfort Daniela. Or himself, for that matter. The Rider team had a solid plan, but that was no guarantee of success.

Mica had pulled favors to borrow a client's private jet for this trip so that Daniela's burned identity—Celeste Rivera—wouldn't show on any commercial passenger manifests and betray her Atlantic departure and place of origin. The sleek, dual engine Gulfstream could hold ten people, but currently only carried four passengers—him and Daniela with Rafe and Reece seated a row back. The ride was smoother and quieter compared to the plane Jackson and Rafe had stolen to escape Colombia.

Daniela had been mostly silent since leaving Justin behind. Jackson had reassured her that he trusted Mica, but his words hadn't seemed to pierce Daniela's despair. Under her silence was a remarkably strong woman who'd stayed alive in a cartel family, had the audacity to testify against her uncle, and survived three days on the run with Justin to reach Atlanta for help.

Beside him, she stared blankly ahead, looking lost. In profile, even somber, she was beautiful. She wore her hair up, with loose curls dripping down. Unsure how to comfort her or how much comforting she wanted, he held her hand.

"Do you trust me, Daniela?" he asked.

"I wouldn't be with you if I didn't."

Her statement wasn't a yes, and Jackson felt like he needed better confirmation. He wanted to talk about having a relationship now that they were alone, but they had the more immediate issue of preparing for tonight's meeting. He didn't want to add to the stress of leaving her son and the cartel reunion with his desires.

Jackson continued, "We'll be working closely together, and sometimes I might make demands or change the plan. All only with your safety in mind. I need to know you trust me."

"I trust you." She gave a humorless chuckle with a small shake of her head. "You may be the only man I have ever trusted, which is a sad reflection of my life, since we'd spent less than forty-eight hours together in my twenty-seven years before I came running to you for help."

"You deserve better." He resisted the urge to tell her he could be that something better. He wanted to make life easier and safer for her in the long term, but declaring such a thing would conflict with his preceding rational thoughts he'd expressed to Rafe about how he would get to know Daniela first.

He glanced back at Rafe and Reece, another Rider employee. Rafe was twirling his harmonica in his hand while Reece leaned back, taking a nap. Jackson had a good team for this mission—men he'd worked with before and trusted with his life.

"Thanks for letting me clothes shop at the airport," Daniela said.

"No problem."

"I've never been to New York," she added.

If they were in and out as he hoped, she wouldn't be able to claim to have seen much of the city, but she'd be safe. Perhaps some other time, he could bring her back for a leisurely stay, one she could enjoy without worrying about the cartel or getting back to Justin in a hurry.

"Mica and Claire picked a good location—far from Rider base in

Atlanta and easily accessible by a major airport. Do you want to talk through the plan again?"

"Tell me more about the nanoparticles Claire mentioned."

~

As soon as they landed and Jackson had cellular service, he showed Daniela a text photo from Mica showing Justin and her son playing with the magnetic blocks on the carpet. Daniela felt another wave of gratitude toward Mica and Jackson.

Heart a little lighter, she thanked him, and he passed her appreciation on to Mica. After deplaning, Daniela waited with Jackson and the other Rider employees as their luggage was pulled from the rear compartment.

"Rafe, thank you for coming," she told him.

"Of course." He shrugged as nonchalantly as if he was simply helping her change a tire rather than meeting with deadly cartel members. "This is my first time in New York."

"Me too." She turned to Reece, whom she hadn't formally met, and extended a hand. "Daniela Rivera, formerly Daniela César. Thank you also for coming."

He inclined his head. With the toothpick in his mouth shaded by a thick mustache, a lean figure in jeans and pair of boots, he belonged in a Western movie and not her modern-day nightmare.

"Yes, ma'am. Happy to oblige. Happier to have front row tickets to see a ballsy woman confront her demons." His voice was a slow Southern drawl, like sweet tea thickly poured on a summer day.

Jackson took the luggage from the attendant. They hadn't packed many clothes, but the Rider equipment and guns required larger baggage. She had only her carry-on suitcase resting behind her.

"You think my plan to confront the cartel and convince them to leave me alone will succeed?" Daniela asked Reece.

"Oh, no, Miss Rivera. I don't believe for a hot minute those egotistical sonsadonkeys will take kindly to a request to back off, even appealing to logic." Mustache twitching, he twisted the toothpick between his teeth as his eyes sparkled. "But you'll have the satisfaction of knowing they underestimated you."

Letting Reece's words sink in, she watched him saunter away with luggage in tow to the hangar exit and toward a parked SUV.

Jackson rubbed her shoulder with his free hand while the other rested on his luggage handle. "You ready? That's our rental. We'll drop our things at the hotel and then go to the church. Do you need a bite to eat first?"

She shook her head. Food was the last thing she needed at the moment. It wouldn't sit well on her churning stomach. "I'm fine." She'd been telling herself that little lie for so many years it rolled naturally off her tongue. She was a mess, barely holding on by a frayed thread that could snap at any moment.

Yeah, she was fine.

⁓

BY THE TIME Jackson and Daniela stepped in front of the bronze doors of the church, they had reviewed the plan three times, and everything was in place. Still, Daniela was a ball of nerves.

She tugged at the black three-button vest beneath her black blazer. Mica had loaned the outfit to her, explaining it was made from layers of woven Kevlar, making it bullet resistant. The material was hot for a warm September evening, and Daniela hoped she wouldn't put it to use. The pants that accompanied the outfit were too short for her, so she'd worn her blue jeans instead. Stylish black sneakers with thick soles completed the outfit, chosen more because they would enable her to make a quick getaway if needed rather than for style. In her back pocket was a burner phone Rafe had given her in case she was separated from the Rider team.

Jackson wore a suit of the same material as Mica's. His look was both professional and mouth-wateringly attractive. He stirred emotions and desires in Daniela she hadn't felt since... well, the last time they'd been together.

Reece was outside somewhere, covertly monitoring the entrances and exits of the church and ready to defend the pair of them. Rafe would join Reece, but for now he was occupying the attention of the nun on patrol while Jackson set up equipment at the entrance. She liked Jackson's partners. Somehow, they conveyed calm energy overlaying fearless violence. Rafe had a smooth Latino vibe and Reece a Wyatt Earp flare.

Saint Patrick's Cathedral in Midtown Manhattan was clad in marble interspersed with dozens of stained-glass windows. Spires over three hundred feet tall flanked the main entrance. As Daniela and Jackson entered through the gaping bronze doors and past the open, sliding, glass pocket doors, he plucked the remote control off the floor fan at the entryway.

The ceiling was impossibly high and gracefully vaulted. Enormous columns lined the path along the pews leading up to the altar. When they reached the front of the church, they stood at the altar, admiring the gray-white Italian marble beneath a bronze canopy. Here, the baldachin sloped upward to a statue of Christ.

"Now we wait," she said, wringing her hands.

He stayed protectively close to her, for which she was grateful. "Now we wait," Jackson agreed.

11

———————

A half hour later, when two black Honda Pilots parked out front, Jackson turned on the fan at the church entrance with a click of the remote.

Two men entered, followed by five more, who stood just inside the doors, blocking the exit. In the lead was a tall, thin man in a tailored slate suit. He took in the church before his gaze settled on her. Then he approached with the other bulkier man at his side. The five others remained at the last pew.

"Sebastian," she said, the warmth in her voice drew from childhood memories.

My, how he's changed.

Still thin but all hard angles now without the boyishness of youth. His chiseled cheekbones were sharp enough to cut glass. The luster in his once lovely hazel eyes had gone flat. He'd cut his dark hair short and styled it with a slight wave on top.

"Daniela," he said curtly, pausing at the back pew.

Her heart ached for him—for what life had done to him. He was his father's second in command. What a cruel twist of fate for both of them.

Swallowing, she resisted the urge to step forward and wrap him in a hug. She had known the boy, loved him like a brother, but she didn't know the man.

"This is Diego," Sebastian said.

Daniela stiffened but refused to flinch or retreat. She wouldn't show fear. Fear was a weakness to men of power.

Diego was probably forty and built like a minotaur, with broad shoulders and a wide bone structure on his towering frame. He moved stiffly, as if all those bulky muscles were barely contained energy. His eyes were a chilling, hard, dark brown, almost black, shadowed by a prominent brow line with a permanent scowl. His hair was buzzed on the sides and longer on top, slicked back from his face.

"This is Jackson," Daniela said.

He tipped his head politely and said, "I was raised to shake hands on introductions, but do what you're comfortable with." Jackson left his arm extended several beats, as though challenging the men at civility.

The tension in the cathedral thickened.

At last, Sebastian shook Jackson's hand. "Let's sit," he gestured toward the pews.

They walked to the first row, Jackson again keeping close to her, offering support and protection. Daniela sat to the right, closest to the aisle, and angled her body toward Sebastian, who sat across the aisle to the left. Jackson sat in the row behind her, while Diego sat in the row behind Sebastian.

"It's good to see you, cousin." She said the words warmly, finding the truth in them. She could see him and be reminded of happy memories, despite the sad circumstances of their reunion. "I wish there wasn't this great divide between us." She glanced down at the aisle, which seemed to be a physical representation of the metaphorical chasm between them. "We are both victims of our parents' poor life choices."

Sebastian's gaze softened for an instant before sharpening. "My father has ordered your execution."

Although she'd suspected as much, hearing the words, especially from Sebastian, felt like a cold slap to the face. She took a moment to choose her words carefully. "The damage is done, Sebastian. Nothing is gained by continuing this feud."

"His honor is wounded." Her cousin's voice was flat.

She let out a low scoff. "His pride, you mean. He shot his brother in cold blood, so Hermes damaged his own honor. I restored my father's honor by ensuring Hermes went to prison. His wounded honor?" Heat rose in her cheeks. "He did that himself. Any of his cartel followers can see that."

The twisted irony was that if she'd shot Hermes in retaliation for killing her father, she would have earned the respect of the cartel. Because she opted to send him to prison, she was someone they felt had to be dealt with.

"He believes your death is necessary. That is enough justification for his will to be done. And your death will also send a warning to any who contemplate testifying against the cartel." Sebastian's words sounded rehearsed, devoid of emotion. Had life beat him down with such severity that he would show her no compassion when talking of her own execution?

With a heavy heart, she said, "Then I have nothing more to say except thank you for your honesty and for taking the time to meet with me."

Daniela started to stand, when Sebastian spoke. "His enforcers have been commissioned for this job. *Los Cuatro Jinetes.*"

The Four Horsemen.

Daniela felt the color drain from her face. Fortunately, she sank back onto the hard wooden pew before she could collapse on shaking knees. Jackson must have sensed her distress, because he placed a hand lightly on her shoulder.

Sebastian continued, "The bounty has been arranged to be paid upon delivery of your death."

She squeezed her hands together to keep their shaking unnoticed. Her stomach clawed its way up her throat, but she bit back the urge to wail. "And my son?"

"My father will not suffer vengeance from your son when he becomes a man."

She wanted to lash out at Sebastian, wrestle him to the floor, holy ground be damned. She wouldn't lose her son to these monsters. But Sebastian was the messenger. Unleashing her anger on him wouldn't retract the hit on her and Justin.

Jackson squeezed lightly where his hand rested on her shoulder, as if reminding her she wasn't alone. He'd always represented a steady force in her life, however indirectly. He must be furious, too, hearing someone talking about killing his son. How unjust was life that she'd brought father and son together under such circumstances? But Daniela bore the weight of blame for this part.

"And when I best your horsemen?" she asked, transforming her fear into anger and infusing it into her voice, making it hard as granite.

Sebastian tilted his head to one side as though he hadn't considered the possibility his father's men might fail. He glanced at Jackson as if sizing him up for the task. "Then we end the feud."

Diego started to protest, but Sebastian held up a hand to silence him.

"I will speak to my father about obliging these terms. The cartel will agree that any further expense outweighs the benefit if you beat The Horsemen."

When her legs finally regained their strength, she pushed to her feet. "It seems our meeting has concluded. You will tell any men you have outside the church to stand down. We're leaving."

Sebastian stood. Diego followed but made a gesture with his hand. The five men near the door snapped to attention. Bulges under their jackets indicated they were armed.

"So much for a parle," Daniela said, using the chastising tone she only implemented when Justin made a mess of the kitchen.

On the inside, fear spiked her heart rate. Mica had known the cartel would ambush them, but would the woman's escape plan work?

"Diego," Sebastian said with a growl. "I didn't authorize this."

"But your father did. *No preoccupado.* We'll wait until they are outside the church."

"We will walk free, or you and your men will find yourselves on the ground writhing in pain," Jackson said.

Daniela explained, "When you entered the building, the fan placed at the front blew nanoparticles onto your skin and clothing."

Jackson pushed the remote, and the fan stopped blowing. "They're harmless unless activated, at which point they deliver a debilitating electrical shock. You and your men will wait inside the church for thirty minutes and not follow us. If Daniela and I are attacked or if you leave the church in pursuit of us, the nanoparticles will be activated."

Jackson had explained all of this to Daniela in preparation for this meeting. Apparently, the Rider team had used these nanoparticles on one other occasion to bring an adversary's team to their knees.

Daniela added, "When you get to your hotel, a simple shower and washing your clothes will rid you of them."

"Out," Diego ordered, ignoring their warning.

SEBASTIAN LINGERED behind as Daniela and her security escort walked toward the exit of the church. The possessive way Jackson placed one hand on the small of her back made Sebastian suspect the man was more than a bodyguard for hire. This was indeed the man who had been on the banister all those years ago, yet Daniela had been living alone when Sebastian had found her. He didn't fully understand their connection.

Mixed feelings rolled through Sebastian at seeing his cousin after so many years. She was thinner and possessed more confidence. Motherhood suited her, though it had added darker circles of worry under her eyes. Well, she had much to worry about.

He walked toward the open church doors, not stepping into the daylight. Did such nanoparticles exist? The threat sounded like something out of a science fiction movie.

"Was it wise to tell her about the horsemen? Now she knows what to expect," Diego complained, walking beside him.

"She's powerless to stop them." He pulled out his pack of cigarettes, smacked them against his palm to tighten the tobacco for a slower burning smoke. "Knowing will only escalate her fear, and fear will cause her to make mistakes."

Diego grunted.

As Daniela and Jackson reached the enormous bronze doors, Diego's men flanked them.

"Now, we can kill her. Easy and done," Diego said. The man's motives were plain—win Hermes' approval and receive the promised bounty.

Sebastian stopped and slipped a cigarette in his mouth but didn't light it. "And what of the nanoparticles?"

"They're bluffing."

"Are you willing to take that risk?" Sebastian had known Daniela all their childhood. She never bluffed. She stood up for friends in need, faded into her father's shadow to go unnoticed by his men, and dreamed of a life outside the cartel. But she had never lied.

"Nanoparticles *mi culo*," Diego stepped forward. "Get them in the car, and we'll kill them somewhere without witnesses."

"Don't," Sebastian warned, snatching the unlit cigarette out of his mouth, suddenly sure Daniela had spoken the absolute truth.

But Diego and the men surged forward to seize the woman and her bodyguard.

Sebastian's body erupted in white fiery flame.

Damn fool, Diego.

Sebastian went rigid as he fell flat on the floor and watched Diego face-plant on the concrete beside him. All of their men fell like dominos. Daniela and Jackson stepped over them and back into the church. She cast one last long look of anguish in Sebastian's direction before his world went black.

· · ·

Jackson held Daniela's hand as they sprinted back through the church to the altar, down stone steps behind it, and into the underground tunnels of the crypts. Per his request, Claire had discovered the little escape route when she'd read about the church online.

"Everyone we can see is down," Reece reported in Jackson's earpiece.

This was a relief because they hadn't been sure everyone would be coated with enough nanoparticles to have a stunning effect. Furthermore, Sebastian would have had men who remained unaffected if they had lingered outside the church. Mica had told Jackson about the first and only time Rider SI had used the nanoparticles, which had been through the air ducts in an enemy's building.

Part of him wanted to go back and put a bullet in every single man on the floor for them having dared threaten Daniela and his son. Jackson had never felt such a protective rage in his life.

"Anyone follow us into the church?" Too busy fleeing with Daniela's safety in mind, he hadn't stopped to see if the cartel pursued them.

"Not that I saw," Reece said.

"We might lose contact in the tunnels. See you in the alley."

"Copy that."

They zigzagged before taking a set of stairs up and out into a street under a skylight. Rafe pulled his rental car up to the curb, where Jackson opened the door for Daniela. After she slid in, Jackson joined her in the back seat. When she had her seatbelt on, he moved toward her, enveloping her in his arms. He'd been terrified for her—afraid they'd shoot her on sight or have snipers on roofs when they exited the church. But Reece had reported no unfriendlies on rooftops.

She felt cold and stiff in his arms. Her silence was agony. She must have emotions swirling inside, but she bottled them up. For his benefit or hers? He rubbed his hands up and down her arms, not wanting to probe her feelings in front of the other team members. Later, he could help her talk through this.

"So, how was the chat?" Rafe turned to look at them, voice casual, as if they'd just met with a realtor and not a ruthless Colombian cartel.

"It ended in a half-dozen men undergoing electric shock therapy."

"So it did," Reece said cheerfully, deftly navigating the roads. "Now we know their intentions. And now they know Daniela isn't some helpless damsel in distress. They'll tread more carefully."

"That's one optimistic outlook," Jackson mused.

"It's the best one," Rafe said.

Daniela felt hollowed out, scraped raw by life's hardships. She'd survived the cartel for this long, but the task seemed more daunting than ever.

The car ride was silent, though Jackson's glances of worry in her direction spoke volumes. He looked as though he wanted to comfort her with more than a simple embrace. Tempting as it was to relax into him, she hadn't sought comfort in a man's arms since—well, since she entered WITSEC and Jackson spent the night with her. If she indulged now, she would certainly melt down in his arms. Nobody needed to see that unsightliness. She had to keep herself together until she was alone.

She had followed Jackson through the tunnel system, grateful the man seemed to keep his bearings. Mechanically, she'd put one foot in front of the other until she'd reached the vehicle, paying no attention to the swinging turns Reece made. She was still reeling from the shock of the confrontation by the time they pulled up to the hotel.

Once inside, Jackson escorted her to her room. At the door, she slipped out of Mica's bullet resistant blazer and swiped her keycard over the lock. When the mechanical click sounded, she opened the door.

"Daniela—"

Jackson looked like he wanted to hold her, but she needed time to process the meeting with Sebastian and the news of the Four Horsemen.

"I need to be alone. I need to shower and be alone."

His throat bobbed in a swallow, but he took a step back. "Okay. You've got the burner phone. Call me if you need anything."

"Yeah, okay."

"I'll be back soon with food."

She nodded.

After the door shut, she walked into the bathroom and started the shower, stripping off her shoes and jeans. Back in the bedroom, she flopped onto the bed, buried her face in the pillow, and screamed, letting out all her rage into the cotton. This was how she'd always dealt with emotional turmoil. Let it out. Don't let it eat you from the inside out. When Justin had been an inconsolable toddler amidst a fit, she would go into another room and throw her own fit, often with Tupperware bouncing off walls. Some cultures taught people to bottle up anger and fear and poisonous hate. Her culture taught her to purge her mind and body of those things until she could face hardships with calm objectivity once again.

She wished she had Tupperware to throw. Instead, she slammed her pillow against the bed repeatedly until her arms burned from the exertion. With the anger gone, she was left with despair. Quietly, she stepped into the steaming water of the shower, sank to the tiled floor, and wept in great shoulder-heaving sobs.

12

Jackson picked up take out at a Greek street vendor just down the road from the hotel. He dropped off orders with Rafe and Reece, thanking them again and hearing they'd already debriefed Mica about the church fiasco. Then he headed back to Daniela's room.

She'd been so pale earlier, he hated to leave her, but he wasn't the type to force his company on a woman. She'd said she needed to be alone, so he respected her space even though leaving her shredded his emotions.

He knocked on her hotel room door, but no answer came. He could knock louder or holler, but he didn't want to attract the attention of other guests. Instead, he took the extra key card he had to her room, swiped the door unlocked, and opened it.

"Daniela?" he called softly, not wanting to spook her if she was sleeping. The sight of the bed in disarray had him momentarily panicking. Had there been a struggle here?

Before he could yell out her name, the sound of sobbing came from the bathroom, mixed with the gurgle of running water. Letting the door close gently behind him, he set the takeout bag down beside the coffee machine and knocked on the bathroom door.

The water cut off.

"Can I come in?" he asked quietly.

A sniff was followed by shuffling. When the door swung open several moments later, she was dressed in a t-shirt and shorts with her wet hair up in a towel. Her face was splotchy red and her eyes were puffy from crying.

He stepped closer to her, wrapping his arms around her. "Talk to me, Daniela. Let me help you. Share the burden with me." He rubbed his hands along her back as she relaxed in his arms.

After a moment, she pulled away and looked around the room, a lost expression on her face. "I don't know how to let anyone help. Justin and I have been on our own for so long. I only know how to keep the fear and anger contained until it erupts. Bottling it up like champagne under pressure is what I know how to do until I have the time and isolation to let it pop."

She'd had no one to talk to all these years, Jackson realized. She'd been a single parent in hiding with no support group. Well, she had one now.

"You're not alone. You have me. Tell me how I can help, even if it's only listening."

"Talking won't stop the Four Horsemen from coming. Talking won't keep Justin safe. Talking won't make my uncle end the hunt."

Jackson's heart ached. He wanted to pull her into his arms again, but her stiff body language warned him to keep his distance. He withdrew his hands and rested them at his sides. "No, talking won't do any of those things. But it will help with the stress. It may give you clarity to better manage everything life is throwing at you right now."

"What if it has the opposite effect? What if silence around others is the glue holding me together and talking shatters my reserve? I can't afford to fall apart right now." Her voice held an edge of desperation mixed with anger.

"If you shatter, we'll put you back together. Everyone shatters now and again. It gives us the chance to build ourselves back stronger than ever."

Her eyes flashed as she shoved against his chest. "I can't afford to show weakness!"

"Not even to me?" he shot back, shocked by her sudden aggression and how her lack of trust in him flared his own temper.

"Especially not to you. You worked for the American government. They sold me out. You are the father of my child."

"You came to me for help. Why push me away now? *I* didn't sell you out. I would never jeopardize your relationship with Justin. Give me some damn credit, Daniela." He stalked away, into the main room near the bed, raking a hand through his hair. Did she think he was some heartless bastard who would take away her son?

When he turned back toward her, she was in his face with one fist pounding on his chest. There was force behind the blows but not violent intent.

"Men take what they want, don't they?" she yelled.

The outburst surprised him, but it also felt like progress. Yelling was closer to talking than silence. If she needed to lash out to keep her sanity, so be it. But she'd better be prepared to spar with someone who didn't idly take the abuse.

He pinned her arms to her side, leaning his face close to hers. "*I* don't take what I want. And I'll be damned if I allow you to lump me into the same category as the assholes in your life."

Baffling him, she nipped at his lips. Unexpected arousal shot through his body. He crushed his mouth to hers in a searing kiss as he pressed closer to her. His hands roamed her backside as he lost himself in the desperate and tantalizing motions of her mouth and tongue.

Before he started tearing clothes off, he jerked apart from her. Her eyes were wide, cheeks flushed, and lips swollen from the kiss. He wanted to ravage every part of her in a way that made her scream his name and forget her anger and fear.

"No. Not like this." He took another step back. "I won't be accused of taking what I want in the heat of the moment."

She dropped her hands to her side. "I'm sorry. You're right. That wouldn't be fair." Her voice was calm now, and her eyes had transitioned from angry fire to smoldering desire. "I'm a mess. I'm angry at my situation, and I struck out at you." She lifted her t-shirt over her head and tossed it aside. "So don't take. Give. Give yourself to me."

He gaped at the beauty of her naked body, the perfect swell of her breasts and hourglass waist. "You're exquisite." He didn't move. Couldn't move.

Stepping toward him, she tugged off his jacket and unbuttoned his shirt before pressing her lips to his bare skin.

"Daniela." He sucked in a breath at the heat coursing through him. This woman spun his mind into confusion as the heat of anger transformed abruptly into the heat of passion.

"Let me take what I want." She finished removing his shirt before lightly raking fingernails down his chest as she arched up for a kiss. "I want to take you."

When their lips met, she plundered his mouth. He let her take, matching her fervor as he cupped her breasts, rolling his thumb over them and drawing moans from deep in her throat.

Her hands slid lower, impatiently tugging at his pants. "Off," she commanded in a breathless, heady voice.

He unzipped them, shoving the slacks to the floor. When he raised back up, he claimed her breasts with his mouth. Her hands fisted in his hair as she gasped. He moved up, kissing her chest, then neck, then lips again as he guided her closer to the bed.

"Now," she demanded, hands stroking him with rough urgency.

She tumbled onto the bed, pulling him on top of her, and opened to him, drawing him down, wrapping her legs around him. Digging her fingernails and thrusting her hips, she urged him harder and faster.

He had imagined having her in a long, languid passion, but that could wait for next time. Today, he would give her what she wanted— a violent release to counter the coiled stress within her. Sweating and panting, he pushed to give her what she craved.

When she cried out, pleasure coursed through her shuddering body, undoing his composure. His body erupted in exquisite delight as he emptied himself into her warmth.

· · ·

Daniela's mind felt like it had done a hard reset. As she came back to awareness, her naked body lay tangled with Jackson's. He felt like a warm, safe place of retreat. But she had an ugly world to face, not hide from under the sheets.

Technically, they'd never even made it under the sheets.

"That was wonderful, Jackson."

"Hmm." He drew a lazy finger along the edge of her breast. "Next time, let me take my time with you." He pressed delicate kisses along her neck.

Her body heated all over again. She liked the sound of next time, but a relationship wasn't something she could indulge in right now.

When she had tried to push him away moments ago with hurtful words, he'd resisted. She'd been touched by his persistence and need to help her through her fear, making her emotions abruptly swing from anger to arousal. He'd allowed her to take, and now he was giving more in the form of his embrace, holding her like he had all the time in the world to spend with her.

Now what?

"Talk to me, Daniela. Something is churning in that beautiful mind of yours."

"What can I tell you that you probably don't already know? I'm terrified of the men Hermes is sending after me and our son. I was devastated to see my cousin in that church. Your arms are the only solace I've had my entire life, and I hate how unfair all of this is to you."

"Tell me about Sebastian." Jackson lazily twirled a finger through her hair. His casual post-sex cuddling helped ease her tension.

"We were kissing cousins." At the surprised look on Jackson's face, Daniela elbowed him playfully. "Not really. We kissed once, and that's when we both knew Sebastian's secret. A secret we had to keep from our fathers."

"Did you?"

"For a while." She curled into Jackson. "But Hermes began to suspect Sebastian wasn't interested in women. On his sixteenth birthday, he sent one of his brothel women to sleep with him. I didn't know about his scheme at the time. I was on my way to visit my cousin, bringing him a peanut butter icing cupcake—his favorite. When I barged in..." She closed her eyes, recalling the terror in Sebastian's eyes and the smirk on the gangly woman's mouth.

"The prostitute had obviously deduced his secret, and that gave her power over him. I didn't know what she intended to do with that knowledge, but I had to protect Sebastian. His father would kill him if his suspicions were confirmed. The man was known for his violent fits of rage, often resulting in the brutal death of anyone unfortunate enough to have incurred his wrath." Daniela remembered the outrage she'd felt—the injustice for Sebastian that his father would toss out a test like this with a planted spy as a prostitute.

From Daniela's own selfish perspective, Sebastian was the only friend she'd had in the cartel. She hadn't wanted him to suffer, and she hadn't wanted to lose him.

Jackson remained silent, listening.

She ran fingers along the muscles of his arm and chest, feeling the smooth power of them. "I ordered Sebastian out of the room and whirled on the woman. She was older than me but half my size, and I was the daughter of Alejandro César. For the first time in my life, I threatened someone. I told her she would keep her mouth shut, but she cackled, schemed, and wanted a bribe. That path would lead to never-ending compromises. So, I spoke the language most understood in the cartel—violence. I backhanded her with the promise that if she spilled Sebastian's secret, I'd spill her blood."

"You stood up for him, protected him. Now he's coming after you," Jackson said with a disbelieving shake of his head.

Daniela rolled one shoulder. "I don't know what's happened to him since I left the cartel. I don't know what hardships he's faced. We both lost our only friend when I went into WITSEC. I couldn't even so much as say goodbye to him. To anyone. He probably resents me."

"Resents you've had to live in hiding?" Jackson's warm body tightened around her.

"Resents I had the opportunity to hide. From his perspective, I'm the lucky one who escaped."

13

———

Mica drove Justin to Jackson's house so Daniela could see her son as soon as she was back in town. She had Claire working to gather more information on the Four Horsemen after learning about their enlistment to the cartel's cause.

Mica didn't know how to balance this particular job. Somehow, she was supposed to let these Horsemen come after Daniela as if she was bait and take them down with no one getting hurt.

"Your mom will be excited to see you again."

"Yeah. I had fun though. Allen is pretty cute. I think it would be cool to have a younger brother or sister," Justin said.

His statement conjured images of Jackson and Daniela traveling together. They must be using the time to talk about their future. Even if Daniela didn't want to be romantically involved with Jackson, hopefully she would at least let him be a part of Justin's life. Judging by the way they had looked at each other at his house the other day, flames were sparking, so they may consider a future together.

The mother and son pair must've felt so isolated all these years. Mica couldn't imagine raising Allen without David. She also couldn't imagine what a hardship Daniela's heart must have been through these last two days, leaving her son with a practical stranger. Mica would never do that. No, that wasn't true. If her family was in danger and taking Allen on a trip was more dangerous than leaving him behind with armed protection, she would go without him.

"I heard you talking about the tranquilizer gun with Mr. Rider," Justin said.

"Uh, huh?" She glanced at him in the rear-view mirror but couldn't read his expression. She'd left the tranquilizer at home above her fridge when they'd departed this morning to drive to Jackson's house.

"How does it work?" Justin asked.

"Point and pull the trigger like any gun. Have you ever shot a gun?"

"No. My mom doesn't allow them, or I thought she didn't until I saw she owns one."

"Parents are all about protecting their kids. If we had our way, our children's lives would never be in danger."

Several silent beats passed before Justin spoke again. "Maybe I can see Mr. Rider and Allen again sometime."

Mica parked the car in Jackson's driveway. "We'd like that. You were a real treat."

She exited the car, surveying the neighborhood. No apparent threats. The morning seemed typical suburbia, with the distant hum of a lawnmower and a few people tending their shrubs. Mica was reminded that she needed to sort out a safer long-term place for mother and son.

She carried Justin's duffel bag, filled with everything David had bought for him, and walked close to him along the sidewalk leading to the porch. After unlocking the door with the spare key Jackson had given her, she ushered Justin inside the safety of the house, punched in the alarm code, deactivated it, and plopped the bag on the floor.

Glancing at her watch, she said, "They should be here in a half hour. Make yourself comfortable."

The doorbell rang, sending Mica on alert. Jackson wouldn't have rung the doorbell, but an attacker probably wouldn't either—unless they were trying not to draw attention from the neighbors while getting the home occupants to open the door.

Glancing back, she noticed Justin standing partially behind the hallway corner, watching her for cues. She raised a finger to her lips before motioning for him to hide just around the corner.

Leaning forward, she looked through the peephole to see the top half of a man with dark brown hair, rugged sun-kissed skin, and intense gray irises. He wasn't cartel, with his trim hair, smooth shave, and keen eyes. He looked like a cop.

"Can I help you?" She didn't open the door. Angling her vision down, she didn't see a weapon in his hand but couldn't be certain there wasn't one hiding under his worn leather jacket.

"I'm DEA agent Nash Rucker. I'm looking for Jackson Hart."

Yeah, she wasn't taking him at his word. "I'll need to see some credentials."

"I've got them. Open the door." His voice was gruff and demanding. If he thought he could intimidate her, he was wrong.

"Hold it up to the peephole, Mr. Rucker."

"Agent," he corrected her. Dipping into his jacket, he produced a gold badge and held it up for her viewing.

"Give me one minute to make a phone call and verify your name." She took her phone out of her back pocket and dialed a number.

Agent Rucker scowled, running an impatient hand through his hair as he paced.

What was his business with Jackson, and why was he so agitated?

"Mica, what's up?" Claire asked through the phone.

"There's a DEA agent at Jackson's door. I need you to make sure he's legit. Name's Nash Rucker."

"One moment, please." Clicking sounded on the other end of the phone. "Yep. Legit. I'll send over a picture so you can verify."

The picture popped up on Mica's phone. DEA. She sighed.

Time to add another layer of complexity to an already jacked up situation.

"I am opening the door, Agent Rucker."

As soon as she opened it, the tall man with broad shoulders

nudged his way inside, looking around. Mica blocked him from further entry, even though he was a foot taller than her. She'd brought down men his size, and they didn't intimidate her. This close, she noticed circles under his eyes like he hadn't slept, or hadn't slept well.

"Where is he?" Rucker demanded.

"That's as far as you go, Agent. Jackson Hart is out on assignment."

Rucker snorted. "What kind of assignment does a washed out FBI reject take?"

"My assignments." Mica said coolly. "He works in private security."

"I need to talk to the son of a bitch. My partner's in a hospital bed because of that asshole."

"I find that hard to believe, but if you'd like to sit down and have a civilized conversation. I'm interested to hear what happened."

"Are you hiding him?" He tried to move around her again.

"If you won't be civilized, I'll have to ask you to leave."

"Look, lady." He grabbed the lapel of her jacket, eyes popping wide when he spotted the gun in the holster. "Oh, shit."

He entered fight mode, but Mica was already there. She'd seen he was a loose cannon the minute he stepped inside the house without an invitation. She had a boy in hiding to protect and wouldn't hesitate to reign in a DEA agent who thought he could plough through her.

He grabbed for her with both arms, clearly thinking he could subdue her in a bear hold.

She ducked, pivoted, and slid out of the jacket in his grasp. Twisting the material around his wrists, she restrained his hands as if tied with rope.

He snarled and struggled. "I don't hit women."

"Good for you." She lashed a leg out, kicking him solidly in the side. "I do hit jerks who barge into my employees' houses with no warrant and a bad attitude."

He let out a whoosh of air, his face turning shades of angry red to purple.

Mica held the jacket tight, preparing for her next move to release it, spin behind him, and go for the ever-painful kidney punch to bring him to his knees. She hadn't started in this business working behind a desk and would never tolerate being pushed around.

The color drained from Nash's face as he blinked several times. His sharp eyes lost their steely focus. When he drifted to his knees, she let loose the jacket, confused.

"Wh—what?" he said, eyelids closing.

Did he have a medical condition? Was he fainting? He was too young for this to be a heart attack or stroke.

When he collapsed on the floor, she saw Justin standing behind Nash, holding the tranq gun with shaking hands.

Oh, sh... sugar.

"Ah, well," she let out a short, nervous chuckle. "Now we know the tranquilizer works."

Dang. She hoped Nash Rucker still had a pulse when the medication wore off.

She walked toward Justin and plucked the weapon out of his hands. "I'll take that." It had five more darts, and Mica didn't want one accidentally landing in her thigh.

"Was that you looking out for me?" She bumped an elbow playfully into Justin to lighten the mood and his terrified look as she slipped the gun in her back waistband. When he pulled his eyes away from the man on the floor and looked up at her, she added, "Thanks. But we're going to need to chat about stealing."

He must have taken the gun after David had stored it above the refrigerator. She had a lock case for her personal weapon but not Claire's prototype tranquilizer.

"Are you going to tell my mom?" Justin sounded frightened now, not like the kid who'd just played hero to subdue a threat.

"Tell you what. I won't mention to your mom you stole my tranq gun and shot someone, if you don't mention how I didn't lock up my tranq gun to keep an eight-year-old from stealing it and shooting a DEA agent."

"Okay. What are you going to do with him?"

She looked down at Nash Rucker as she pulled out her phone and dialed a number. "Are you in town? I need you to pick up someone."

"Alive or dead?" the male British voice asked.

"Alive. Of course, alive." *Yeesh.* She didn't kill people. "I need you to stash him somewhere until he and I—" she hesitated, glancing at Justin, "—can have a friendly chat."

Daniela was quiet in the car on the way to Jackson's house after a stop for groceries, trying to process her emotions. She'd never gone food shopping with a man. The domesticity of it had an oddly comfortable feeling, aside from Jackson being on high alert for any threats.

In the store, he had inquired about what she bought for Justin, curious to know if he had any food allergies and what their son liked and didn't like. The first day they'd spent here, he'd thrown the football with his son and taken a genuine interest in asking about his likes and dislikes.

She had watched the pair bonding only for a few minutes, feeling the pain of sorrow at what Justin had missed the first eight years of his life. So far, Jackson hadn't asked to reveal his identity to Justin or demanded to have a future with him. But based on Jackson's behavior, he wanted one. Perhaps his silence on the matter was him allowing Daniela to adjust to the idea of Jackson taking a future role in their lives.

First, I need to have a future.

Jackson's and Daniela's phones dinged simultaneously. She pulled hers from her jeans pocket.

"It's Claire." She looked at the test message and images. "She sent a conference invite for this afternoon and pictures of the Four Horsemen." Daniela scrolled through the photos. "She'll tell us more on the call." She glanced at the pictures, recognizing only one—Diego Aguilar, the aggressive Latino from the church.

When Jackson pulled into the driveway, Mica's car was parked in front of the garage, which meant Justin was inside, waiting for her. Daniela's heart lifted.

Jackson parked behind Mica's vehicle and slid out of the driver's seat. Grabbing the luggage and an armload of groceries, he headed toward the house.

She exited Jackson's truck and walked around to help carry groceries.

Suddenly, a car across the street slammed to a halt before a thin, short man with a pockmark face, dressed in worn brown leather exited.

Daniela's world shifted to slow motion at the site of Lido Perez —*El Chupacabra*. She'd seen his face for the first time on the message Claire had sent only minutes ago. A short Latino man with a pock-marked face.

One of the Four Horsemen had already found them.

Daniela's heart thudded mercilessly.

Jackson, who had arrived at the porch with his hands full of groceries, snapped his head up to assess the threat before Daniela could even cry out a warning.

The sidewalk, winding through lush grass and leading to the house where Justin was, seemed to stretch a mile long. The sprinklers kicked on, spraying a fine mist, as they click, click, clicked over the yard.

Daniela turned toward the house, instinctively thinking only of how she needed to reach Justin inside.

El Chupacabra pulled out two guns.

"Get down!" Jackson screamed as he dropped the groceries and reached for his Glock.

Lido wiggled his guns in the air, yelling, "I will introduce you to my friends! Sweet and Salty!" With muzzles pointed toward the sky, he licked the tips one by one.

Thinking only of needing to protect Justin, Daniela sprinted through the yard and toward the side of the porch as Lido took aim at her. She put one foot on the edge and launched upward, hands on the railing, vaulting over it.

Jackson fired, the harsh noise cutting through the tranquil neighborhood. Lido stumbled back and crumbled in toward himself but didn't fall.

Why didn't he go down?

He righted himself and fired rapidly as he ran toward the porch.

Jackson dove at Daniela, taking her down flat on the deck yet somehow protecting her from the fall at the same time. Wood splintered around them from the rain of bullets.

Eyes fixed on her attacker, Daniela gaped when Lido slipped on the wet sidewalk, falling forward. As one last gunshot settled in the air, his body stilled. A stream of red ran through the cracks in the flagstone and into the grass before being washed away by the sprinklers.

She and Jackson sat up.

"He shot himself in the head when he slipped." Daniela stumbled over the words in disbelief. When she looked up, Mica stood in the doorway, gun drawn.

Above Lido's body, a thin rainbow shimmered in the water droplets as the sprinklers continued their steady click, undeterred by the dead body on the lawn.

Jackson helped Daniela onto a pair of shaking feet as Mica stowed away her gun.

"*Mierda*. You're bleeding." Daniela raised her hand but didn't touch the gash on Jackson's head where crimson flowed steadily out of the wound, along his blond hair, and down onto his shirt. Leaning against the house for support, she felt her head rush as her stomach rolled.

"I'm okay. It's a graze."

Mica had her phone out, barking orders. "Rafe, how far out are you from Jackson's? Get here and take Daniela and Justin to Reece's place. They can't be here when the cops arrive. I'll explain later. Daniela, take what's already packed and go with Rafe."

When Daniela opened her mouth to protest, Mica persisted, "The police will have too many questions we don't have time to answer. You need to get out of here. We'll patch up Jackson. Don't worry about him."

Swallowing back emotions, Daniela nodded and rushed toward the house to see her son. When she spotted him in the foyer, she bent and wrapped her arms around him for a fierce hug, relief rolling through her even knowing their safety was only temporary.

"We're leaving now. Your things are still packed?" She noted the bag on the floor as she pulled back from him.

Justin nodded. "We're running again?"

"No. Hiding somewhere else. I'll explain later."

"Is Mr. Hart coming?"

She liked that Justin trusted him, felt safer with him.

She kissed her son's forehead. "Yes. He'll join us."

14

Jackson winced but remained still as Emergency Room physician David Rider, Mica's husband, sutured Jackson's scalp where Lido's bullet had clipped him. Jackson had met David a few times and was grateful for the medical care.

Meanwhile, the police interviewed Jackson and Mica. Boss and employee told the same story, leaving Daniela and Justin out of the picture.

"Why do you suppose this man targeted you?" Detective Wake asked. He was the third person to run through questions, many of them similar. He wore slacks and a button-down shirt under a blazer. Probably in his mid-forties, he had crow's feet and a receding hairline lightly streaked with gray hairs.

Jackson held an ice pack against his scalp. "I'm former FBI and I work in private security now. I've probably made enemies along the way." He didn't mention knowing Lido was a cartel hitman. The police could uncover that for themselves.

"Your story seems to check out. There will be a full investigation."

"Yes, sir. I understand."

"From the angle, I can see how he accidentally shot himself. If ballistics confirms that, you'll be cleared."

"Thank you."

Detective Wake continued, "You shot the intruder directly into his bullet resistant vest and the shot wasn't fatal. There will still be an investigation because you discharged your firearm in public... a neighborhood. I doubt you'll face charges, as it's clear from your house damage—and your head—that he attacked with deadly intent."

Jackson nodded.

"I suspect, working for an investigative group like..." he glanced down at his notes, "Rider Security and Investigation, you'll do your own digging into the provocation behind today's attack."

"Yes, sir."

The detective stood and handed him a business card. "Share with me anything you uncover."

Jackson stood and took the card. "That go both ways?"

"Not necessarily."

Shortly after the detective left, the crime scene investigators also departed. Jackson changed out of his bloody shirt for a clean one, then began loading his truck with Daniela's bags, along with all the groceries they'd just bought. He wanted to see Daniela, run his hands over her after today's scare. His head pounded from the shot and the tedious hours of questioning. He should also probably eat something today.

Mica trailed behind him. "You're good to keep working this job?"

"It's not a job to me, Mica." His look and voice were equally hard.

"Yeah, I got that." Her voice carried the same clipped tone as his.

He dumped the last bag in the back of the extended cab, closed it, and turned toward her. "I'm sorry for snapping. You're doing me a solid on this one with my family. I'm okay. My head is still in the game. Literally." He pointed with one finger at the bandage on his head. Beneath it, the wound throbbed mercilessly. He hoped the acetaminophen David had given him would kick in soon. He'd declined anything stronger, not wanting a substance that might cloud his judgment or slow his reflexes.

The game was already afoot. Four hitmen. Four Horsemen. One dead. He'd imagined orchestrating their arrests, but dead worked too.

Visions of bullets flying and zipping too close to Daniela had his gut clenching. They'd talked about her obeying his command, yet she hadn't heeded his words to take cover during the shooting. Frustration and anger gnawed at the edges of the lump of fear in his chest. Losing her today had been a real possibility. If he blinked too long, he visualized her in the gunman's crosshairs. How were they going to survive this nightmare?

"I thought we had a little more time," Jackson told Mica, "but Sebastian and Diego must've tracked my connection to Daniela before we even met with them at that church. One of the Four Horsemen couldn't have gotten here so soon after the New York rendezvous if they only just learned about my relationship with Daniela. They had inside information."

"I have an idea about that." Mica's lips drew in a thin line. "A DEA agent showed up here asking questions. Asking for you."

"DEA at my house? What did he want?"

"Something about his partner being in a hospital bed because of you."

"What?" Jackson jerked back. "I didn't put anyone in the hospital."

"I know that, which is why we need to question him."

"Okay. Where is he?" Jackson wanted to see Daniela, but he wanted answers more.

"I had Dorian pick him up and take him to a... remote location for questioning. I also moved his motorcycle into your garage."

"You've piqued my curiosity."

"We'll talk to him, then you can join Rafe and Daniela at Reece's place. He's got good security. You'll stay there until we sort out a plan to trap the next incoming Horseman. You and Rafe at all times with Daniela until this is over."

"Thanks, Mica." Between giving him a job and real purpose in his career and now helping him with his family, he owed a debt to this woman he could probably never repay.

"Keep in mind that because the cartel might have a mole in the US government somewhere who knows about your relationship with Daniela, we don't tell authorities. Not even Eddie."

Jackson nodded. His friend at the FBI would be furious later to learn he'd been kept out of the loop, but Mica was right—either the US Marshal service, the FBI, or the DEA had leaked information about the connection between Jackson and Daniela.

DANIELA WALKED through Reece's house to calm her nerves and make a mental map of the layout. Outside, privacy trees surrounded his ten-acre property, making it feel secluded and peaceful even though they were on the outskirts of Atlanta. Inside, it had an enormous master bedroom and bathroom with a walk-in closet and three guest rooms. An actual library was complete with a rolling wall ladder. The kitchen had an island and a six-burner stove.

She found Justin in his new temporary room and joined him on the bed. Earlier, she had taken him around the back of Jackson's house, then to the driveway to leave with Rafe in order to minimize chances Justin would see the body and blood in the yard. Still, he'd heard the shots. So many shots.

Santo Dios, she could still see Jackson's blood flowing out of his head. Nausea hit her all over again at the memory.

"I'm sorry we had another scare today." She stroked a hand through Justin's soft brown hair.

"You left to talk to the cartel. I guess they said it isn't over?" His blue eyes gazed up at her.

"Diplomatic negotiations failed. Do you remember when I told the fairytale of the princess and the king?"

Justin nodded.

"You understood it wasn't really a fairytale. You understand how that story is the story of our past?"

"I know, Mom." His matter-of-fact tone and eye roll had her smiling.

"I think it's a little less scary when events sound more like stories instead of our own lives. So, I'll tell you this next part like a story." She stroked a hand over his head. "The evil king's brother wanted to fully take over the throne after he killed the king, but he was forced into exile. There, he could only exert his influence remotely. He blamed his exile on the princess and sent his men hunting for her. Always hunting. Even though she was living in hiding, they found her. She confronted the son of the king's brother, her cousin, explaining how she wanted only peace and to be left alone. She didn't want trouble, and she didn't want the throne. But the exiled brother's heart of stone only fixated on revenge." She sighed. "And the rest of the story has yet to be written."

"More bad men will come after us?"

"A few more, yes. I'm sorry."

He frowned. "Enemy goons."

"Enemy goons," she confirmed.

"We're not living a fairy tale," he said.

She nodded, the heavy weight on her worried heart sinking a little deeper. "Perhaps my analogy is faulty."

"More like *Star Wars*," Justin said. "We're the rebels and the cartel is the evil Empire. How would you write it, Mom? If you were ghost-writing the princess's story, what would it look like?"

She smiled warmly. "Four wicked henchmen—or maybe bounty hunters like Boba Fett—with hearts as black as Darth Vader's cape, were sent after the princess, each with the same task—to exact the leader's revenge. But the princess had wits, and she wasn't alone. Enlisting the help of a prince and his friends, together they defeated every person sent after them. And the princess and her son lived happily ever after."

Justin's brow furrowed in a puzzled expression. "Don't the prince and princess hook up in all fairytales?"

Ah, cáscaras. Shucks. He had her there. In fact, the prince and princess had already "hooked up" before the happily ever after was certain. She didn't regret the night with him, never would, but ending up with Jackson might be as much wishful thinking as the two of them defeating the four assassins. Three now.

She could write the ending with her and Jackson together, but she wasn't ready to contemplate a long-term relationship with a man she had romanticized about for entirely too long.

"I suppose the prince and princess usually do share a happily-ever-after. But, as you pointed out, our story is more like *Star Wars*, so maybe they don't."

And the prince had been shot. Jackson had been shot because of her. Because of the danger she'd brought right to his front door.

JACKSON FOLLOWED Mica's car with his truck. They'd taken separate vehicles to the industrial district in downtown Atlanta and now parked in front of a warehouse, where he followed Mica inside. Judging by the layers of dust and cobwebs, the place was not in use.

Dorian, the suave Brit in Mica's employment whom Jackson had worked with on a previous assignment, wore a suit and stood beside a man seated in a chair. Dorian nodded a greeting to the pair of them.

A hood hung over their captive's head. His arms were restrained behind his back, bunching the sleeves of his leather jacket.

Mica had explained DEA Agent Nash Rucker's behavior leading up to her restraining him. Apparently, Jackson's son had played a role, shooting someone in the ass with a tranquilizer dart. Jackson had taken that little nugget of information with a mixture of pride and abhorrence—something he could process later, perhaps when he had to tell Daniela.

"Everything okay here?" Mica asked Dorian.

The man nodded calmly as Rucker unleashed curse words.

Ignoring her captive, Mica told Dorian, "Thanks for your help."

Dorian placed a key in Mica's hand, taking his dismissal casually, then turned on his heel and left. Mica waited until he was completely out of view before she pulled the hood off Nash's head. Because of this silent exchange, Nash had neither seen nor heard Dorian, so his part in Nash's abduction remained anonymous.

Nash blinked several times. "The fuck is the matter with you? You kidnapped a federal agent."

"And you assaulted a civilian," Mica reminded him. She had no intention of reporting him. Something so tedious would take time from more pressing matters.

"I barely touched you."

"Why don't we let both of our actions slide? You asked to meet Jackson Hart. I bring you Jackson Hart. You're welcome."

Rucker looked him up and down. "What the hell happened to your head?"

"Lido Perez. *El chupacabra.* You're lucky Mica took you away from my house. There was a shootout there today. Lido's dead. I'm guessing, as a DEA agent, you know who he was."

"One of the Horsemen. Why is the Colombian cartel after you? And can we have this fucking conversation without cuffs?"

Mica walked behind him and unlocked the cuffs.

Jackson crossed his arms. "Your colleague warned you someone was coming for me? Who is your partner, and how do they know me?"

"Rita Jones knows you from an undercover job." When Rucker said the name, Jackson's eyebrows lifted.

"I haven't seen Rita since..." He shook his head. "In years." He'd almost said since the woman had called him to convince Daniela Cesar to join WITSEC and testify against her uncle.

Rucker rubbed his wrists and rolled his shoulders. "Somebody knew you two had worked together, and they beat the hell out of her to get your name."

Jackson frowned. "I'm really sorry to hear that. Will she be okay?"

"She's got fractures and will need physical therapy and shit. I don't know if she'll ever be able to go back to work."

"Sounds like the cartel thinks they have some type of score to settle with me." Jackson certainly wouldn't give this man any details about Daniela. "You might want to keep your distance, Agent Rucker."

Nash's phone rang. He reached for it but hesitated, looking back-and-forth between Mica and Jackson.

Mica shrugged. "You can answer that. You're not a hostage."

"Could've fooled me," he grumbled.

Mica crossed her arms. "Your behavior signaled hostile intentions, and therefore you were subdued peacefully, without threat of any ill health effects, like broken bones. We moved you here to have a civilized conversation. Because I didn't know if you were going to be civilized, I needed to move you out of a peaceful subdivision."

Rucker looked like he had another smart retort and didn't like being accused of hotheaded behavior which could be seen as a threat to bystanders. Instead, he answered the call. "Rucker. Shit. Yeah... I'm on it. I'm on it. I'll be there." He disconnected the call and ran a hand through his hair. "I'm supposed to pick up my niece from her field trip. Where the hell are we?"

"Let's go," Mica said with a gesture of one arm. "I'll drive you there. I've got water and a protein bar in my car." When he shot a look suggesting no way in hell would he get in the car with her or trust her with any interactions involving his family, she added with a shrug, "Or you can catch a ride share. No skin off my back."

He looked around the warehouse, jaw clenching. "I'll take that ride, but this isn't over."

Mica quirked her lips as if she'd expected such a reaction from an officer of the law. "Jackson, I'll text you later. Go take care of your family."

15

———————

*D*aniela was sipping tea in the kitchen when Jackson's truck pulled into the large circle driveway. He'd taken hours to make it from his place to Reece's—a drive that was only thirty minutes. He'd sent a text letting her know he'd finished police interviews and had to take a detour with Mica.

Rafe and Justin were playing a video game in the entertainment room. They were both sufficiently distracted that her pacing had gone unnoticed.

Daniela walked out to help Jackson carry grocery bags inside the house—the same groceries they'd purchased earlier that day. As seemed his habit, he'd parked the truck facing the road. She understood the position was for easier escape if needed.

His skin was pale, and a bandage clung to one side of his head, held in place by gauze wrapped circumferentially. He looked exhausted, so she held her tongue.

"I can take care of this," he said.

"I need something to do."

"Justin is okay?"

"I explained the situation to him," Daniela said. "I'm walking a fine line between wanting him to be appropriately scared and cautious without terrorizing him. I won't gloss over events and pretend everything is copacetic."

"I'm sure he's smart enough to understand you're still being hunted and a killer closed in on you today. It's good you're being honest with him."

He didn't make eye contact as he spoke, and she wondered what she'd done to upset him. Well, she had her own mind to speak about events earlier.

He dragged the luggage into the entryway while she set the grocery bags on the counter, then they went back to the truck, retrieved the rest, and returned to the inside of the house.

"I'll make steak and potatoes for dinner," Jackson said flatly.

Daniela felt the tension in the air like a humid Colombian sunset after a rain shower. Was he angry with her?

In what universe does that make sense?

Unable to hold her temper any longer, she whirled on him in the kitchen as he placed lunch meat in the fridge. "Don't you ever put yourself between me and a bullet like that again." She kept her seething tone low.

He scowled at her, cheeks reddening.

She continued, shoving hands at his chest. "I asked for your help to stop the cartel from killing us. That does not include killing yourself for me." She was shaking now, picturing his blood flowing down the side of his head. She'd always envisioned him as the quintessential indestructible lawman. Even if he was no longer FBI, he was still *that guy*—the Captain America ready for another round.

Seeing Jackson bleed had made her heart threaten to explode. *Ah, Dios*, an inch closer and the bullet could have killed him.

The bullet meant for me!

Jackson got in her face, matching her anger with his own. "When I tell you to get down, you get the hell down. Not run toward me."

"I was running toward Justin."

"Who was safely inside the house with armed protection," he snapped back.

"When there's danger, I will always think first of my son."

"You can't protect him if you're dead. When I say down, you hit the dirt!"

"Don't tell me what I can and can't do!"

He was right. Because she'd been thinking of Justin and ran toward the house, the bullet meant for her came close to killing Jackson. If Lido hadn't tripped, he could have killed both of them because Jackson had been too busy playing human shield to take the shot.

"Don't tell me I can't do my damn job and protect you."

"I didn't hire you to get you killed!"

She shoved him again, needing the space he seemed determined not to give her.

"You didn't hire me, Daniela."

He was right, of course. Mica had refused to take payment, explaining how the Rider team looked out for each other's families.

"I'll find a different private security team to help." She spun away, but he snatched her arm in his hand.

"The hell you will!"

When she turned back to face him, he pulled her close, a possessive move her body liked entirely too much.

Her voice shook. "I can't see you hurt. I can't see you bleed again." Hot tears welled in her eyes. "Not because of me."

"Not you." His voice was still harsh. "None of this is your fault."

Stretching up, she pressed her lips to his and threw her arms around his neck, riding the wave of anger and fear straight into passion.

Jackson kissed her back—hot and hungry, like a beast staking his claim. With arms wrapped around each other, their mouths plundered. All of her fear and anger at events today pooled like smoldering lava in her. She hiked one leg up and around him, wanting him closer. Wanting him merged with her.

"Mom?"

She and Jackson broke away instantly. Cold flooded her body at the loss of Jackson's proximity, and her mind resumed functioning again.

"Sorry, honey. We were arguing," she said.

Justin had never seen her kiss a man before now. She had to suppress a laugh at the look of disbelief in his eyes. He wasn't naïve enough to believe the two adults had only been arguing.

"Hey, bud. I'm sorry," Jackson said, looking stricken.

Daniela laid a hand on Jackson's cheek with a soft smile. "We Colombians are passionate people, Jackson. Most of us don't quietly suppress our feelings while calmly disagreeing with someone. My son isn't intimidated by a little yelling. We were still communicating. When arguments degrade to name calling, that's when the situation is out of control."

Justin walked around them to the fridge and pulled out the orange juice bottle. "I think you should add kissing to the list. When arguments degrade to kissing, that's when the situation is out of control."

Daniela laughed as a stunned Jackson leaned on the counter, looking like he needed it for support.

She playfully tousled Justin's hair. "I'm going to go take a bath," she tossed over her shoulder as she left. She needed to clear her head.

She'd never had these wild mood swings, like a pinball darting from fear to anger to passion and back to fear. She'd certainly never shared such spiking emotions with a man before now.

Jackson leaned on the counter for support, trying to grasp what had just happened. His head had been aching, between the gunshot wound and meeting the DEA agent with Mica, when Daniela verbally pounced on him for putting himself in the line of fire.

Arguing had morphed to kissing in a flash. That woman's body stored a well of passion. Surprisingly, he liked her version of arguing, because it showed how much she cared. Nothing in his relationship with his ex-wife had ever been so heated—the disagreements or the physical attraction.

He regretted Justin had witnessed his fight with Daniela, though. Jackson had never yelled at a woman before now and didn't want to set a poor example for his son.

"I'm sorry about yelling at your mother. I was worried about her, but I shouldn't have raised my voice." The last thing he wanted was for Justin to fear him or to feel unsafe in this house.

Justin, who'd been rooting around for a glass, found one and poured the juice. He shrugged. "She was yelling at you. She yells at me sometimes." He gulped his orange juice.

"I would never hurt her."

Justin snorted. "I'd be more worried about you in a physical fight."

Jackson blinked at him, then grinned at the boy's nonchalance. "Why is that?"

Justin slid into the seat at the counter and leaned in conspiratorially. "She knows how to fight. This shady place we lived in before the house had all these bad dudes. 'Trolls trolling for trouble,' Mom would say. She walked me to and from school every day."

Jackson's skin prickled at the thought of Daniela and Justin living in a dangerous neighborhood. Never again, he vowed.

Justin continued, "Sketchy dude comes up to us wanting cash and jewelry—like, who carries cash anymore, right? He had a knife, so I'm thinking we're going to make a run for it. Mom's fast. She always catches me at tag."

Jackson nodded, entranced by the story.

"Instead of running, Mom whips out a can of mace and—bam!—dude's blind and wailing. But she doesn't stop there, no. She smacks him upside the head with her purse, and lemme tell you—that thing's heavy." He drank down the rest of the juice, smiling at the memory.

"She's a good mom." Jackson straightened, warmth spreading through him.

"Yeah. She's a keeper." Justin set his empty glass down on the counter. "You wanna throw the ball again?"

"I do. First, I need to situate dinner in the oven so it will be ready and on the table by the time your mom's done with her bath. Do you know how to set a table?"

16

$\mathcal{D}$inner passed amicably, though Daniela found her appetite lacking as visions of *El Chupacabra* flashed through her mind.

Rafe kept the conversation going with talk of sports. Jackson asked Daniela about her work—ghostwriting and insurance claims. She was grateful they kept the focus away from the day's events.

"The insurance claims pay the bills. The writing pays for fun."

"Do you ever struggle for ideas or creativity?" Jackson asked.

"I love fairytale retellings. The concept is already there, but I take creative twists."

They made quick work of the cleanup, with Rafe and Justin clearing the table, Daniela rinsing dishes, and Jackson putting them in the dishwasher. Here was another first for her—tidying the kitchen with a man. She liked Jackson in her space, whether grocery shopping, cleaning, or even arguing.

When Justin was situated in the game room. Daniela made her way to Reece's library, where Rafe was setting up his laptop with a projector and the drop down screen from the ceiling near one wall.

"How did they find us at your house?" Daniela asked as Jackson brought cups of steaming tea. She already felt betrayed by the

Marshal service. Surely, someone on the Rider team wouldn't have leaked that information, and she wouldn't start the conversation with accusations.

Jackson handed her a mug of tea as he sat beside her on the couch. He breathed in the steam rising off his cup as though stalling for a moment to pick his words carefully. "Do you remember the woman from the party I was with when we first met? The woman I accompanied to the party?"

"I remember you said you were her escort."

"Yeah." He sat beside Daniela.

"And then later, we met again when she wanted me to testify." Daniela recalled thinking Rita Jones was a bully but didn't bring that up. Something in Jackson's tone suggested that wasn't relevant.

"Yes. She's DEA. A cartel man beat her up to get my name. Someone remembered I had a conversation with you that night and thought it was an avenue worth pursuing to find you."

Daniela shook her head, sadness welling inside her. She held the teacup with both hands, breathing in the smells of lavender and chamomile. "Sebastian. Only he would have even noticed me talking to another man. And only because he once cared about me."

"I'm sorry you lost a friend in your cousin when you escaped the cartel."

So, Sebastian had recalled the night, and he'd had agent Jones tortured for information about Jackson. No, Daniela didn't know her cousin anymore. This calculating, cruel creature was someone else entirely.

When the video feed began, Daniela stiffened on the couch. Jackson set down his tea and slipped a warm hand into hers. On the screen, Claire sat at the end closest to view with a keyboard in front of her. Mica sat across from her.

"Thanks, everyone, for gathering," Mica began. "Claire is going to fill us in on what we're up against. The Four Horsemen."

Claire took a sip of her water before launching into the research she'd done since the conversation Daniela had with Sebastian. "The first one is Hermes' longest standing henchman—Diego Aguilar. He's wanted in six countries for murder, probably all sanctioned by Hermes. He started his illustrious career with armed robbery before working for the cartel. His weapon of choice is a Beretta 96 A1 he had painted gold and calls *Pepe*."

"He was the one with Sebastian at the church," Daniela said.

"Next up is Lido Perez, also known as *El Chupacabra*." The photo on the screen showed him with his two guns and a cold glee in his eyes. "He was actually kicked out of a Columbia gang notorious for kidnapping tourists for ransom because he enjoyed killing the tourists. Bad for business. He's been a horseman for about four years, since replacing one who died in a cartel battle. But he's also the one who shot himself on Jackson's lawn today."

One of four already eliminated. That he was dead from sheer chance—his bad luck and her good fortune—didn't offer Daniela much comfort. The other three wouldn't be so careless.

Claire flipped the images to two men dressed in cargo pants, muscle shirts, and black glasses. "Armando and Emile, two other Horsemen, usually work together on jobs. They're known for their stealth. With six years in the Venezuelan military, they know their way around weapons and demolitions. Armando is also a cyber-criminal, aka black hat—someone who hacks for data theft and malicious intent."

"What color is your hat?" Daniela asked Claire.

Claire grinned, as though she appreciated Daniela taking an interest. "I was a hacktivist—cyber attacks for ideological reasons—in my younger days. Now, my hat is gray, meaning I have ethical reasons for hacking in the interest of protecting our vulnerable clients, but I'll switch to malicious intent if the situation calls for it."

"Four men," Mica said.

"Four nightmares," Daniela countered. "I've heard of these last two men. Their body count is legendary."

"Survive three more, and you're free," Jackson said.

"So long as my uncle stays good on Sebastian's word."

"It's this or back to witness protection," Mica said.

Daniela shook her head. "Sebastian will keep his promise. That's what matters. Defeat The Horsemen, and the cartel won't spare further resources trying to eliminate me." She sipped her tea. "Easy as pie."

"We need planning. Planning and keeping our wits. Ready to fight and ready to flee. If we let our fear rule us, we'll make mistakes."

Daniela felt Mica's words of caution and wondered if they were directed at anyone besides her. This didn't seem like a team burdened by nerves, but her hers sure as hell were frayed.

DANIELA TUCKED JUSTIN INTO BED, taking the time to read a Rick Riordan book from Reece's library. After a few chapters, she quietly lingered beside her son, even though the terror of the day's events still had her wound tight. Ever since her father's death, life felt like one long string of borrowed time. The Horsemen were riding hard toward her with razor-sharp blades to sever that tenuous strand.

She wanted so much more for Justin. When she noticed he'd fallen asleep, she set the book down on the bedside table. Wiping at a tear on her face, she steadied her resolve. *Wise men say to spend each day like your last. Well, not like this. Not in fear.*

They would best the demons after them, and she and Justin would be safe. And she would be free to love Jackson if her heart continued to lead her down that path.

Quietly, she made her way back to her room and crawled under the covers. Like an insatiable adolescent, she wanted to sneak into Jackson's room and find solace in his arms.

The blood-pumping, sizzling passion he stoked in her was unlike anything she'd ever known. She couldn't look at him without an invisible pull to be close to him. She also couldn't look at him without feeling the dreaded danger she'd put him in by seeking his help.

If she went to him in the night, would they make love? Would he think she gave herself to him as some manipulative move to secure his help and loyalty? Cartel life had taught her that every action had an ulterior motive. Maybe she did have a motive. Being with Jackson took her away from her reality. In his arms, she could envision a life together. But was indulging her desires and feeding her imagination fair to him?

Her mind swirled through these thoughts, wondering if she should talk to him about a hypothetical future together. Then again, if her happily ever-after scenario didn't play out, she would be asking him to leave his life behind for her. That wasn't fair to Jackson.

At last, her eyes grew heavy, and she slipped into a restless sleep.

"*EL CHUPACABRA IS DEAD*." Sebastian resisted the urge to smile even as he said the words to his father.

Daniela had always been crafty and resilient. Sebastian admired her, even if she was his father's current whim, about whom Sebastian was forced to follow orders.

From his confined prison chair, Hermes scoffed. "Lido was an idiot. I'm not surprised he failed."

"Three more, and this feud is over. I gave her my word."

"Not mine," Hermes bit out the words.

Sebastian wanted to lean over the prison table and shake some sense into the old, bitter man.

"The men talk of the futility and danger of further drawing out your revenge. Already Diego..." Sebastian searched for the words that wouldn't be revealing to any authorities listening. Diego had beaten a DEA agent to within an inch of her life for information. The recklessness could have scathing repercussions. The animal needed to be put on a leash.

"Diego does what must be done," Hermes said mildly.

Sebastian clenched his teeth, wanting to point out that his father was being the idiot. "At this rate, the entire alphabet soup of US agents will bear down on us. I have more important things to be doing."

"More important than your father's will?"

Sebastian pursed his lips. He was doing his father's will. Every.

Damn. Day. He kept the business running. He balanced the books, paid employees, and laundered money. These things were more than enough work for one overlord.

Killing Daniela? That was his father's obsession. An ill-tempered mistake the man wanted to rectify with no real purpose. The longer Hermes stayed behind bars, the more he seemed to lose touch with reality and rational thought. He'd always been pig-headed and self-centered with a taste for violence, but isolation seemed to magnify his egomania.

How long before the old man turned on his only son?

"I am still doing your will," Sebastian reminded him. "I fly out to speak with the duo tomorrow."

Armando and Emile were already researching and planning to go after Daniela, because all Horsemen had been simultaneously notified of the contract on her life. They wouldn't be so easily dispatched as Lido. Daniela and Jackson would never see them coming.

17

"Thanks again for loaning us your home," Jackson told Reece over the phone as he tugged on a clean shirt for the day. He set the phone on speaker onto the bathroom counter.

"My pleasure. Whenever Mica confiscates my house for Rider jobs, she sends Jess and I on vacation, so win-win. Mica's only ask on this one was that I stay close in the event my services are required again for your case. I voted for a bed-and-breakfast an hour north surrounded by some great hiking trails, but Jess picked the Ritz-Carlton and a spa day."

Jackson envisioned both and found he could be happy at either location as a vacation spot if Daniela and Justin were with him.

"You find everything you need okay?" Reece asked.

"Yeah, man. This place is quite the setup."

Reece had a library he'd built with his wife, Jess, in mind. Out back, a hot tub with full privacy awaited use. Its presence had Jackson envisioning Daniela in a bikini, skin glistening wet as steam rose around her. That image had kept him awake last night, but no way would he sneak into her room like a teenage boy. He wanted her to feel safe with him and not worry he'd come knocking for a tumble under the sheets.

"You read the security features?" Reece asked.

Jackson loaded toothpaste on his brush. "Driveway alarm. Security alarm. Motion-censored external lights. Arsenal behind the hidden panel in the library. All that's missing are sentry guns and a bomb shelter." He started brushing his teeth.

"All of my security is legal, so sentry guns are out. I could work on a bomb shelter though... maybe by the back shed."

Jackson shook his head, though Reece couldn't see it. Around his toothbrush, he said, "Word of the day, chimera. An impenetrable security compound is a chimera—as illusive and mythical as the Greek, fire-breathing monster with a lion's head, a goat's body, and a snake's tail."

"Well, if Bellerophon can kill a chimera with a spear, you can get Daniela out from under the cartel." Reece gave a sober *tsk*. "I'm sorry you're going through this, man. This is a rough way to have a family dropped on you—finding out their lives are in danger."

Jackson spat and rinsed his mouth. "Yeah. Thing is, I don't know if Daniela will want a family with me when this is over. We have all the chemistry—always have—but will she choose me?" He set his toothbrush down on the counter. "I don't know. I want to maximize my chances, but I don't know what I'm doing." Jackson wasn't sure why he was confiding in Reece. They hadn't been on many missions like he had with Rafe, but he wanted another opinion, or maybe just emotional support.

"Hell, man, none of us know what we're doing. There's no manual for the confabulations and consternations we suffer, especially in romantic relationships. If you feel like now is the time to go all in, then you'd best do so."

Jackson tried to absorb the encouragement as he wet a rag and lathered it with soap.

Reece continued, "I figured I'd lost my chances with Jess. She wanted more than I was ready to give. When horrible circumstances threw her back in my path, no way I was letting her go again. Determinedly and doggedly, I showed her and convinced us both I was worthy of a relationship."

"All in." Jackson inspected his head and gently cleaned the wound with the soapy rag. Because Daniela was upset by his injury and the wrap-around gauze would be a reminder, he didn't reapply the bandage. It looked smaller this way.

"If you love her, take the bull by the horns. Carpe diem. Don't let the opportunity slip away. Don't look a gift horse—"

"Yeah, yeah. I got it. Thanks, Reece."

"Anytime."

"Enjoy that vacation." He disconnected the call.

AFTER BREAKFAST, Jackson and Daniela took a walk around Reece's property—both as exercise and to discuss egress routes both by car and by foot.

When the basics were covered, Jackson slipped his hand into hers. "This okay?"

She glanced back at the house, wondering if Justin was observing them. They'd left him watching *Rebels,* so his attention was probably fully consumed.

"It's okay," she told Jackson, enjoying the warmth of his touch. "It's nice, actually."

They walked in silence, dew laden grass crunching beneath their feet.

"I thought about coming to you last night." She bit her lip.

"I thought about visiting you as well." He squeezed her hand. "I didn't know if you would worry about Justin finding us."

"We both made the right choice. I would have worried." She leaned against Jackson. "I want him to know you're his father, but our situation is so volatile. What if we have to vanish into hiding without you? It would crush Justin, gaining a dad days before ripping him away."

"I would follow you, Daniela. If leaving became my only way to stay with you and Justin, I'd do it."

The mix of hope and worry bubbling through her threatened to overwhelm her. "You have a work family and a job here." She tried to pull her hand back, but he held firm.

"You're my family. I haven't brought up this topic because you're managing a lot now and I don't want to add to the pressure. I would follow you, Daniela. You and Justin are my family," he repeated. "If you'd have me."

She swallowed the lump in her throat and forced tears to subside before they could pool under her eyes and fall. She was thrilled to hear he wanted them and terrified this blossoming relationship would be too fragile to survive the chaos of the cartel.

She took a steadying breath. "My intention wasn't to make you choose between your life here and one in hiding with us. I didn't know where else to go for help."

"I'm glad you came to me."

"Let's see what happens before we agree on life-altering courses," she said.

"Okay." He brought her hand to his lips and pressed a kiss over the back of it. "But you're welcome in my bed anytime, even if only to sleep."

His offer was so very tempting, so very wonderful, but she didn't want him committing to anything he may resent her for later.

AFTER LUNCH, Jackson took Justin outside for shooting lessons with Daniela's permission. Jackson stood on Reece's ten acres of manicured back lawn, shotgun in hand, pointed at the ground. Trees flanked them on three sides, with the house behind them.

"Most important. You're either pointing the end of this thing at something you intend to shoot or at the ground. Safety first. You need to know your weapons to use them—which guns have a safety and how many bullets they hold." He placed his foot near the pedal to operate the clay pigeon thrower.

Justin stared at him with rapt attention.

"I'm going to trap shoot with a twelve-gauge shotgun," Jackson explained. "Same concept as skeet shooting in that you're trying to hit a moving target—a clay disc, sometimes called a pigeon—launched into the air."

He had already detailed the rounds it held and how to reload it. He wanted to show the boy a variety of weapons for a variety of purposes. Justin needed to know the danger of each of them and that Jackson was capable with any of them. He wanted his son to feel secure and be able to sleep at night knowing he was guarded by a man with calm skills. He wanted the boy to see different types of weapons all handled with the type of respect firearms demanded.

"Okay, eye protection on and earmuffs in place." Jackson wriggled his safety equipment in position with one hand, holding the shotgun in the other with the barrel still pointed to the ground.

Justin donned his protective gear.

Gripping the shotgun with both hands, Jackson said, "Pull!" and pressed the pedal. The clay pigeon shot out at forty-five miles per hour, flying at a fifty degree angle into the clear blue sky. He squeezed the trigger, and the orange disc exploded. He cried 'pull' again and repeated the maneuver. He did this until all five shells were spent, then lowered the shotgun.

"Okay. Rafe is here for this next part. He'll stand next to me and slingshot a clay disc into the air, aiming for a steeper angle about twenty yards out. We need a closer, slower-moving target to hit with a 9mm as opposed to scatter form the shotgun."

Jackson set down the empty shotgun, leaning it against the pigeon shooter. Rafe stepped forward, wearing his earmuffs and eye protection.

"Pull!"

Rafe fired the slingshot, and the disc launched into the air.

Jackson drew his 9mm and fired sequentially five times for each of the five clay pigeons Rafe shot.

"You didn't hit any," Justin said as he pulled down his earmuffs.

"Oh, ye of little faith." Jackson winked at him and holstered his weapon.

Justin trailed behind him as they walked to where the clay discs rested on the grass. He picked up all five and showed Justin where he'd hit the target. "Shotgun scatter will shatter the clay in the air. Bullets go right through the clay when it's a single, high-speed projectile."

"You hit five out of five."

The reverence in Justin's tone stroked Jackson's pride. He wanted to be the kind of man a boy might look up to, but he also wanted to make Justin feel safe. He wanted his son to know that if Jackson was anywhere within firing distance of someone trying to hurt him or his mother, they were protected. Now, more than ever, he saw the value of the training he had acquired through the FBI. Stopping criminals was one thing. Protecting his family was another.

"Now. Your first weapon for learning gun safety," Jackson said.

Rafe stepped forward, producing a pellet gun.

AFTER SHOOTING LESSONS, they walked back into the house, Jackson carrying the shotgun and Justin carrying the pellet gun.

"What's your favorite *Star Wars* show?" Justin asked.

"I like the original movies and *The Mandalorian.*" Jackson placed the shotgun and pellet gun back in Reece's cabinet. He kept the 9mm in his conceal carry waistband.

"Did you see the originals in theaters?"

"Uh. I'm thirty-three. I wasn't born when the originals were released." Did he look that old? No. Probably to an eight-year-old, adults aged thirty to fifty were just categorized as much older. Jackson remembered being in elementary school and asking his dad what Vietnam had been like and his dad explaining how he'd been a toddler during the end of the war.

"What's your favorite *Star Wars* show?" Jackson asked, closing and locking the gun cabinet.

"*Rebels.*"

"I don't know that one."

"You're missing out. It's the best."

"Who stars in it?" Jackson asked, enjoying the discussion with Justin.

"I don't know all the voice actors' names."

Voice actors? "It's a cartoon?"

"Animation," Justin corrected.

"Ah, I don't watch those." Jackson couldn't recall the last time he watched cartoons—er—animations. Not since childhood.

"Ever?"

"No."

"Only a Sith lord speaks in absolutes."

"Ah." Jackson chuckled. "Well played. Tell me about this *Rebels* show."

Maybe Justin would rewatch it with him. Jackson envisioned relaxing on the couch with a bowl of popcorn, enjoying television with his son. He hoped such an indulgence would be part of their future.

18

"Hey, bud, while your mom is working, you want to help me with dinner?" Jackson asked.

He had listened to an hour long summary of *The Rebels* from Justin as they picked up after shooting practice. Now, he definitely wanted to watch it with his son.

"Sure. What're you making?" Justin asked.

"Smoked salmon. Does your mom like salmon?"

"Yeah. We've had salmon before. I don't know about smoked. She put hers in the oven."

"We're going to smoke it on the grill." Jackson covered the fish with three layers of seasoning on top—salt, then garlic, then pecan rub.

"It smells good."

"Then we're off to a good start. Do you like salmon?"

"It's okay. I like these breaded fish sticks my mom gets better."

"Let me guess. You douse it in catsup?" Jackson asked.

"Yep."

"How about this? Try one bite of my salmon where you savor the full taste of the flavoring you at least think smells good, and if you don't like it, we can drown it in catsup."

Justin chuckled. "Yeah, okay."

After a moment, the boy asked. "Do you like my mom?"

"Uh. Yes." The discomfort of the boy's stare wormed its way under Jackson's skin. "Yes, I do. That's one reason I want to keep both of you safe." He looked down, focusing on smoothing the seasoning into an even layer over the fish.

Would this turn into a grueling session where the boy asked him on a scale of one to ten how much he liked his mother? Ten. Definitely a ten, and Justin didn't need to know that.

When Justin didn't press for more details, Jackson cleared his throat. "We'll steam broccoli and serve the meal with a side of garlic bread. I've got the loaf over there. Can you cut it open, and we'll smear some garlic butter on the inside?" He hesitated. "Can you... Are you allowed to use a knife? Are you safe using a knife?" Jackson honestly had no idea.

Maybe eight-year-olds weren't supposed to use knives. Goodness, he needed to get a manual. Or just ask Daniela. She probably was the manual. He stretched into his mind for memories. At eight years old, he'd been carving pumpkins. Probably safe. Maybe.

Justin snorted. "I know how to cut bread. I help mom cook sometimes. Besides, I cut my own bagels for breakfast."

"Very well, cut away. The long, serrated knife will be the best to use for cutting the loaf of bread, but that's probably what you've used on bagels. Maybe we can have bagels one morning. What's your favorite cream cheese?"

"Strawberry."

For a moment they worked in silence, Jackson finishing spreading seasoning over the salmon, while Justin mangled the loaf of bread. Jackson didn't mind. He understood learning was a process, and as long as Justin wasn't risking any fingers, he could let the boy figure out how to cut the bread in half. It would still taste good, even if it was uneven and the insides a little shredded.

"Follow me, my good man, and we'll return to the bread in just a minute." Jackson picked up the spatula and the platter with the uncooked salmon.

Justin followed him outside, where Jackson had the grill prepped and waiting.

He lifted the lid. "Now, this is your standard Weber grill, but you turn it into a smoker by pushing all the hot coals to one side, toss in a little pile of pecan wood chunks to add a little flavoring." He slipped the salmon off the tray and onto the side of the grill, away from the smoldering coals.

"Now what?" Justin asked.

"Now we close the lid and let the magic happen."

AN HOUR LATER, they were seated at the table.

"This smells wonderful," Daniela said as she fixed a plate of food for Justin and herself.

"Justin was a big help," Jackson said, prepping his own plate.

"How did the skeet shooting go?" she asked.

She had worked hard most of the day, holed up with her laptop. At least, Jackson hoped she was productive and not isolated in her room worrying. When she'd emerged to join them for dinner, she'd appeared relaxed, so Jackson took that as a sign she'd been focused on work and not the cartel.

"Good," Justin said. "Mr. Hart let me shoot a pellet gun, and I even got to hold the shotgun."

Mr. Hart? That made Jackson feel old. He was glad his son had manners, but Jackson would prefer his first name to be used. Truthfully, he wanted to hear how 'Dad' sounded.

Justin continued, "The gun is heavier than expected. Heavier than the..."

Tranquilizer gun, Jackson thought. He'd forgotten to tell Daniela about that. If it came out now, her rightful temper would ruin dinner.

"The what?" she prompted Justin as she tasted the fish.

"Than I expected." He filled his mouth with a bite of salmon.

When he finished the bite, Jackson changed the subject. "I was thinking we could have a game night tonight. I found a few in Reece's living room."

"That sounds fun." Daniela speared a piece of broccoli and ate it.

"What's the verdict on the salmon?" he asked Justin.

"It's okay."

"Okay? *Es divino*! Divine!" Daniela declared.

"Catsup?" Jackson asked Justin.

"Definitely."

Jackson couldn't help but smile. Catsup on salmon for his son. Duly noted.

MICA WAS READING *The Lorax* to Allen when she heard David come in downstairs. She finished the Dr. Seuss book and kissed his forehead, then descended the stairs to find her husband in the bedroom.

"Hey, hon." He gave her a quick kiss and a smile.

She wanted to hug him after his twelve-hour shift but knew the rule: he liked his scrubs—and whatever blood disease might be on them—off and in the wash before his family touched him.

"Can I get you anything?" Mica asked.

"I'll take a glass of the cab we opened last night. Thanks."

She slipped away, fixed the drink, and found him in the bathroom naked and adjusting the water temperature of the shower.

Admiring the view, she handed him a glass of wine. "Long day?"

"Yeah." He took a sip, gave her another kiss, then stepped into the shower. "Pile up on the Grady Curve, and we took some of the trauma victims from the crash. We had a good team, though. Mackenzie was in the ER with me. Jenna was helpful in moving out pneumonia and heart failure patients to her ICU to make room for the traumas. Rico and Raymond were on EMS transport."

As David talked, Mica thought of the difference in David's mood since going part time. He enjoyed his work more with three twelve-hour shifts per week compared to the four or five before Allen was born. And when she'd met him, he'd been working six twelve-hour shifts in a week.

"How about your day?" he asked.

She watched him lather and wash through the glass partition as she leaned on the counter.

"Justin and Daniela are at a new location. I told you about the horseman." When she paused, he nodded. "There are three left. I've got Claire working to find them. I prefer a proactive approach to reactive."

David scrubbed his hair. "Makes sense. Get them arrested before they get close to your client."

"Exactly. A pair of them live in a boat, but with one being a hacker, Claire thinks she can get a lock on him through his IP address with enough time." If Mica could trace their boat, she could send that information to Special Agent Eddie Finch of the FBI and have Armando and Emile arrested. The key was finding them before they found Daniela.

David exited the shower and toweled off, then stalked to her, crowding her as heat radiated off his body. "Now that I'm all clean, do you have any plans for tonight?"

She grinned as she grabbed the towel around his waist and used it to pull him up against her. "I plan to get you dirty, and you'll need another shower."

He leaned down and kissed her with hungry passion.

JACKSON SET up the board game and read the instructions out loud for everyone. He wasn't familiar with the game he'd found in Reece's coffee table, but Settlers of Catan sounded straight forward—roll the dice, get resources, build settlements. They placed their starter pieces on the board.

"First person to ten points wins. Youngest player goes first," Jackson said, settling on the floor across the coffee table from Daniela.

"It says that?" Daniela asked.

"No, but that's a long-standing Hart family rule."

"I like it." Justin rolled the dice.

Six.

"Your mom gets an ore and a sheep." Jackson, who'd taken the role of resource distributor, handed her the cards representing the resources. When their hands brushed, their gazes locked, and they smiled at each other. "Looks like your mom will score several resources every time a six or a nine is rolled."

"Strategy or luck?" Justin asked, passing the dice to his mom.

"Strategy, of course," she said, playfully batting her eyelids.

Gone was the knit brow worry she often wore. Jackson enjoyed the light in her eyes and the curve of a smile at game playing. Justin, too, looked happy and relaxed as he surveyed the board.

After several rolls of the dice around the table, and trading of resources, Jackson noted, "If I didn't know better, I would think you two are ganging up on me."

Ignoring his comment, Daniela said, "I'll trade you two bricks for an ore."

Jackson glanced down at the cards in his hand.

"You can't do that!" Justin cried. "She'll be able to build a city. That's an extra point. Then she'll only be two points away from winning."

"I find myself torn between my desire to play competitively and the urge to give your mother whatever she wants." Jackson scratched his chin, avoiding eye contact because the comment carried the weight of his earlier statement to keep the three of them together as a family, even if it meant drastic changes to his life.

In what seemed like a gesture of reassurance, Daniela placed a hand on Jackson's shoulder and patted gently.

"That's not how the game is played," Justin protested. "We each play to win."

Jackson grinned at his son but didn't share his sentiment that succumbing to his urge to give Daniela whatever she wanted might still be a win. Maybe he'd even earn a goodnight kiss for his chivalrous behavior. He made the trade, even against further protests from Justin.

"I'm getting two bricks," Jackson countered. "Two more wood and I can make the longest road. Then I'll take the lead."

He glanced at Daniela, whose gaze shifted between him and Justin, carrying the same brimming affection, making Jackson's heart swell.

The game progressed steadily as they laid roads, raised cities, and expanded armies. They bartered and bargained, taunted and teased, each out to win. Mostly, Jackson wanted the fun more than the win. He wondered what a routine family game night would be like.

At last, Daniela rolled a nine and won wheat. She combined that with her ore resource cards, built a city, and reached ten total points.

"Whoop! Whoop!" She pumped her hands in the air.

Justin made a disgusted noise at losing but quickly shrugged it off and laughed at his mom's celebratory jig. She scrambled to her feet and pulled Justin into a hug. Turning her head, she reached back and snagged Jackson's sleeve, dragging him into the group embrace.

Jackson would gladly lose every game to her if it brought Daniela a few blissful moments of joy.

Sebastian stared out of the window as the chopper blades thumped mercilessly above him on his way to Emile and Armando. They were a deadly duo. Stereotypes had the cartel running through the jungle dressed in camouflage clothing with AK47s strapped to their chest. Armando was nothing like that. With his sophisticated intelligence, he used his wits and his fingers to subdue adversaries. Sebastian thought of the Rider SI nanoparticles. Perhaps he'd tell Armando about that clever, incapacitating ploy.

He and Emile had used stealth drone bombs to kill more cartel enemies than most cartel members. In fact, probably only Diego had a higher body count, but only because he'd been around so long.

The brute sat beside Sebastian on the helicopter, no doubt scheming his own victorious path to slay Daniela. The beast smelled of cheap cologne—a revolting scent capable of instantly inducing nausea. Loyal to his father, Diego was forever Sebastian's devious shadow—part bodyguard and part warden to Sebastian's cartel prison.

Sebastian thought back to his first meaningful interaction with Armando almost a year ago.

He had retired to his room after the sun set, leaving behind the rowdy partygoers by the pool. His father's house in Santiago de Cali in eastern Colombia was always bustling with guests.

Sebastian never had a moment's solitude. He ought to be accustomed to the parties after all these years, but still he longed to be left alone—in a manner of speaking, because he couldn't have the type of companionship he preferred. He would take solitude and poetry over the company of the cartel any day.

A gentle wrapping at his door interrupted Sebastian's thoughts. He stopped unbuttoning his shirt and reached for his Walther PPK, keeping the gun behind his back. A man ought to feel safe in his family home, but that had never been the case for Sebastian.

"Who is it?" His hand rested on the doorknob.

"Armando."

Sebastian's brow furrowed as he swung the door open. They were acquaintances moving in the same circles, not friends who paid social visits. "What are you doing here?"

Ice-blue eyes greeted him, ablaze with lust. Armando's gaze slid from Sebastian's mouth, down to his partially unbuttoned shirt and back to his mouth again. "I feel like we've been dancing around our attraction," Armando began, easing into Sebastian's room.

Angst flared in Sebastian as his gaze darted to the hallway. Had Armando noticed him admiring? If he had, had someone else? The other possibility was that Armando had been sent to play a role and trap Sebastian into disgracing his father.

No one makes a fool of me.

Playing it cool, he stepped aside to allow Armando into his room. The man had smooth bronze skin and a face of gorgeous, sharp-angled cheeks and jaw, with a narrow nose. Sebastian made a show of placing the weapon in his hand on the nightstand.

Armando's eyes widened, evidently surprised Sebastian had greeted him with a gun in hand.

Good. He understands I'm not one to trifle with.

"You've misinterpreted," Sebastian said coolly. "There is no attraction."

Armando blinked and looked stricken. "I don't understand."

His pout drew Sebastian's gaze to his lips. Anger flared in him. Who had sent this man to trap him, and how was Armando so convincing?

Sebastian surged forward and roughly backed Armando into the wall. He pinned him there with his arm across his neck. "You put your life at risk coming into my room thinking you can seduce me. Who are you working for?"

"No one. I mean, the cartel, as you know. I'm sorry," he choked out the words. "I thought... I thought sometimes the way you looked at me in passing over the years meant something."

Keeping Armando fixed with one arm, Sebastian checked him for weapons with the other.

"I thought we had chemistry, so I thought I'd take a chance," Armando said, offering no resistance to the restraint and search. This close, he smelled like minty aftershave.

Sebastian searched the man's expression for falsehood. The infiltrator was either very good or very sincere. In a flash of frustration and desire, Sebastian gave in to the attraction he claimed didn't exist. His roaming hand moved over warm skin as he pressed his lips to Armando's.

Hours later, that night had ended with Sebastian's knife to Armando's throat as he threatened his life should he speak of their intimate night to anyone.

Armando's throat bobbed in a swallow. "I understand the danger I exposed you to in coming here, and I'm sorry for that. I'm not sorry about our night. I hope you don't make it our last."

Baffled, Sebastian had released Armando and pulled his knife back. He replaced his blade with his lips. Never had he lost control like this. His survival demanded unfailing composure, not risking everything for an impossible relationship.

He was and would always be as lonely as Robert Frost *Stopping by Woods on a Snowy Evening.*

> *He gives his harness bells a shake*
> *To ask if there is some mistake.*
> *The only other sound's the sweep*
> *Of easy wind and downy flake.*

THE JOSTLING helicopter rattled Sebastian from his memories. He'd never risked another night alone with Armando. Why torture himself with pieces of a relationship he could never have?

19

After playing Settlers of Catan, Jackson's eyes blurred as he read through the information Claire had gathered on the César cartel. They profited from embezzling, intimidation, extortion, and murder. Those who opposed them, including politicians, police officers, and reporters, were assassinated. With a network of planes and pilots, they snuck in billions of dollars of cocaine to other countries.

Jackson thought of Sierra's rescue. She hadn't been kidnapped by the Colombian cartel, but perhaps the plane they'd stolen belonged to them.

Word of the day: bugbear. A source of dread or irritation. The César cartel was a monstrosity of a bugbear threatening to destroy a family Jackson had only just discovered.

"You look like me when I've been writing on my computer for too long." Daniela placed a hand on his shoulder as she offered him a cup of tea. "You should take a break."

"Yeah. I should." He took the tea and pushed away from the desk. "Thanks." Outside, the sun had set. Daniela must have tucked Justin into bed by now.

"What were you reading?" she asked.

"Claire's summary on the cartel. Diego Aguilar is a ruthless S-O-B."

She sat on the sofa and tucked her legs under her. "I'm ready for all of this to be over." Her lovely chocolate hair spilled over her shoulders, and loose waves framed her face. Her skin had a dark golden glow from the lamplight.

He rose and moved onto the couch beside her, needing to offer comfort. When he sat, he set the mug of tea down on the side table.

"Daniela." He placed a hand over hers, resting them both on her leg.

Leaning forward, he kissed her, tender and slow. She opened to him, tentatively inviting more. He took his time, enjoying the taste and feel of her mouth, then leaned back slowly. As much as he wanted her in his bed, he wanted her in his life long-term more. Accomplishing that objective would take conversation, not seduction.

"I want a future with you," he said. Their conversation earlier felt unfinished. Maybe he was pushing, but he sensed her reluctance had more to do with not wanting to disrupt his life than not wanting him to be a part of hers.

She stiffened, eyelashes shuttering down over her eyes. "I don't even know if I have a future."

"I—"

"Tell me about your ex-wife."

If Daniela had wanted to cool his sexual appetite, she'd succeeded. Maybe that had been her goal, or maybe she needed to hear what hadn't worked and how he and Daniela would be different.

He scooted away a little on the sofa, giving her the space she obviously wanted. "I was married for four years. She was a couple years my junior in the Bureau when we dated. We just seemed to click. Everything I was interested in, she was interested in. Movies, hobbies, types of food. I thought, this is what finding your match feels like. Looking back, I don't remember any red flags, except that we should've dated longer. And getting involved with someone who works for the same organization as you can get messy. I'll get to that part."

He ran a hand through his hair. "Six months into the marriage marked the end of the honeymoon phase. All the little lies she told started to crack. The shell peeled off, messy, like an ill-timed, hard-boiled egg. Chip, chip, chip. She pretended to share common interests. I'm not even sure why that was. I guess some people want to be liked, so they feign interest."

He sipped his tea before continuing. "The unveiling was disheartening but not insurmountable for mending a relationship. I tried to tell myself I should be flattered she thought she had to play a role to woo me. We could still make this work, I told myself. You can have a relationship with someone and not have all the same interests. In fact, who wants all the same interests?"

Daniela slid closer, her silent attention encouraging him to divulge all. He'd never discussed these personal events with anyone.

"Chip, chip, chip," he said, staring at the books on shelves across the room. "Most crushing was that she didn't have any interest in having a family. I couldn't recall the exact conversations from when we dated, but I'm sure we both talked about looking forward to having children."

When Daniela leaned toward him, he wrapped an arm around her and she rested her head on his shoulder.

He continued, "Anyway, after a lot of bickering and frustration, and even a few months of separation while I wrapped my head around this different woman I'd actually married, I resigned myself to what our marriage was and not what I wanted it to be. I wondered if some part of the failed courtship was my fault. Had I set an expectation she thought she had to meet?"

He paused, glancing at Daniela and thinking about how talking to her felt so easy. Her expression held interest without judgment.

"People can still be happy without children." He cleared his throat. "But after we aired all our differences, and we were definitely not having children, we slipped into our own worlds of work, both traveling for jobs and widening the gap. Still manageable, right? Look at Rafe and Dia. They make time for each other between their work and it's magical. We didn't have any magic, but there was still time for it to happen."

He blew out a puff of air. "I was fooling myself. I came home early from my work assignment and found her cheating on me with one of our colleagues. I went through all the stages of grief rather quickly—anger, fear, resentment, and acceptance. Skipped right over denial. Those feelings zipped through me in the five minutes the adulterers took to scramble to get dressed. Acceptance came in the form of relief. I had an out. She cheated on me, and I didn't have to feel bad about going our separate ways."

Shifting his weight, he rubbed the back of his neck. "But when you date someone in your workplace and that workplace is the morally incorruptible FBI—or so everyone wants to believe—and your ex-wife tells everyone you cheated on her, the workplace becomes... awkward. Of course, they believed her—I was the one around whom rumors of sleeping with the cartel's daughter were still spoken in hushed tones near water coolers. I'd been getting shit assignments for years because of my *sordid* past. When accusing stares were added to the mix, I left. And I've never looked back. I've never been more satisfied than in my current job."

Daniela smoothed a soothing hand over his chest. "I'm sorry you were mistreated because of our nights together. I never told anyone."

"I know. I don't blame you, and I wouldn't trade those nights for anything." He gripped her hand. He wanted to seize the tender moment, but the past reminded him about Rita Jones and his meeting with Nash. Jackson hadn't filled Daniela in on that detail, and he wanted no secrets between them. "I need to inform you about someone I met with after Lido's death. You asked me the other night how the cartel learned about me so fast, and I told you they had forced the information out of Rita Jones. I know this because I talked to a DEA agent named Nash Rucker who showed up at my house the morning we were back from New York and at the grocery store. He's why it took me even longer to get to Reece's place after Lido's death."

Jackson would omit the part where Mica kidnapped him and left him tied to a chair for hours until they could question him. In Mica's defense, she hadn't known Lido would arrive and the police would question them for so long.

She nodded. "Is he upset with me?"

"Oh, he's pissed but not at you per se. He doesn't know we're hiding you, but he might dig enough to find out. We'll deal with that when it comes up."

"Okay."

"There's one more detail you need to know." Jackson cringed. "When he showed up at my house before you and I arrived home, he demanded to see me. Mica said he became hostile."

"Oh."

"Justin was hiding, but when Nash attacked Mica, Justin shot Nash with Mica's tranquilizer gun."

"He shot a gun?" Bolting upright, Daniela pushed off Jackson. "How did he even get his hands on it?"

"Mica had the situation under control, and she feels bad Justin stole it from above her fridge. She had her 9mm locked but not the tranquilizer gun."

Daniela was quiet a moment before her expression softened. "He's like his father. Brave. He stood up for Mica—whether she needed it or not." She chuckled. "No mother wants to think of her son holding a gun—even if it's not lethal—but it's reassuring to know he'll defend himself and others."

"You've raised a great kid."

She smiled, leaned forward, and kissed him. Tongues mingled in languid, savoring fashion. He cupped the side of her face as he poured his affection into that kiss.

Pulling back, he smiled. He had won that goodnight kiss after all.

～

SEBASTIAN SLID out of the helicopter as the blades slowed. He was exhausted from traveling, having flown from the New York meeting with Daniela back to Cuernavaca, only to hear of Lido's less-than-shocking failure. He then flew to California to see his father, followed by a helicopter to Armando and Emile's yacht on the US East Coast.

The cartel paid the assassins well to afford a boat of this caliber— a blending of opulence and technological prowess with its sleek and contemporary design combined with a helicopter landing pad crowning the upper deck.

How nice for them.

To live port to port in luxury. The only demands of life were the jobs they were hired to do, which they still mostly completed remotely. Sebastian supposed when you had a unique skill set, you could charge enough money to own a multimillion dollar yacht.

Daniela's bodyguard service had their own elite hacker. Sebastian had read about her and all the Rider employees after their clever, shock-inducing nanoparticles. He'd had one of the cartel's information specialists compile a dossier.

Claire Maltisse had been a protégé, rising from poverty to an MIT acceptance at seventeen. She was there only a year before the administration expelled her after she plead guilty to charges of hacking pedophiles' computers and installing software to transfer funds from the men's bank accounts to charity organizations. Clever woman with a score to settle with society. He would bet those skills and that mentality made her perfect for Rider SI.

Now, her skills were about to be pitted against the deadliest hackers Sebastian knew.

He walked with Diego into the bowels of the ship, past an opulent interior adorned with plush furnishings, gleaming marble accents, and panoramic windows that provided breathtaking vistas of the surrounding ocean. Spacious lounges, a well-stocked bar, and elegant dining areas offered the perfect ambiance for socializing and indulging in the lap of luxury. A zing of jealousy coursed through Sebastian. How many men had Armando wined and dined here?

Zero, came the answer.

He was a prisoner like Sebastian.

Armando sat before a computer console of an unparalleled level of sophistication. He had a thick head of black curls, longer than the last time Sebastian had seen him, with matching dark brows above pale eyes framed by crimson glasses. The lenses had a faint blue hue Sebastian suspected were to protect his eyes from endless hours looking at computer screens.

The duo's reputation was legendary, but if Emile thought Armando's relationship preferences would hurt their reputation and business with the cartel, Emile would end him.

Armando's ice-blue eyes were as piercingly breathtaking as they had been on their night together a year ago, stirring emotions Sebastian had worked hard to suppress. His lingering gaze had heat spreading into Sebastian's cheeks, and Sebastian forced himself to look away.

Emile was lankier, with straight hair shaved around the ears and longer in the back. The atrocious mullet-looking nest seemed to connect with tattoos on his neck. Barbed wire or rose vines? Sebastian couldn't tell from several feet away and had no interest in getting close enough to find out.

Emile sat on a love seat against one wall and motioned for the half-naked woman sitting on his lap to stand. He stood as well, slapping a hand on her bare cheek left uncovered by a thong bikini.

Sebastian watched her saunter away. Spies were everywhere, especially in women used and abused within the organization. Sebastian wouldn't divulge his purpose here in front of anyone except the horsemen.

"You want to take a dip while you're here?" Emile offered. He wasn't talking about the ocean, and had obviously misinterpreted Sebastian watching the woman.

Tilting his head to one side, Sebastian said, "No."

"We've a half dozen to choose from. All women though."

Sebastian didn't flinch at the last barb, although Armando did. Nothing could prevent the cartel rumor mill, and the less of a reaction he made to jabs like this one, the less anyone could claim to know the truth. Sebastian resisted the urge to pull out his gun and shoot Emile's dick off. What about just a leg wound? He would never try to get a rise out of Sebastian again, and he'd still be able to do his job on the computer.

Instead, Sebastian replied, "I have three dozen women at home who serve without me having to worry about what STDs they are carrying from you."

Diego chuckled.

Emile took a threatening step forward but halted when Diego tapped a finger on the handle of his holstered weapon.

"A little more tact," Diego suggested, "when addressing the son of Hermes César."

Armando smirked.

Sebastian internally scoffed. Sure, now Diego made a show as if he was all about protecting Sebastian. Diego didn't have Sebastian's interests at heart when he stepped across the church threshold and they were all shocked senseless by unseen nanoparticles. Diego's protection of Sebastian only extended to activities Diego felt fell within the purview of following Hermes' orders. His ever watchful presence mostly waited for Sebastian to make a mistake, especially one that would complete Sebastian's fall from the favor of his father.

"Let's talk business," Armando said, glacier eyes boring into Sebastian, sending heat to his core.

Sebastian dropped his gaze to Armando's mouth before he forced it back to the man's eyes.

He thought again about Armando's offer—whispers in the dark. But words spoken in the shadows couldn't be trusted. Or could they? If Armando hadn't been sent as an infiltrator—and he hadn't been, based on the fact that night had remained a secret—then he'd taken a tremendous risk in approaching Sebastian.

In the end, everyone had barriers in their lives they could never conquer. This would be Sebastian's unfulfilled desire.

"So, Lido failed?" Emile said. "Shocking," he deadpanned.

Diego crossed his arms. "He didn't become a horseman by being a slouch."

"No," Armando agreed. "But you can't pit a *loco asesino* against a security team."

"You'll do better?" Diego challenged.

"Of course. We've already begun our work. Sebastian sent information on the Rider team, and we've been doing a deeper dive. We'll infiltrate Rider SI and root out Daniela's location. We've sifted through IP addresses researching the cartel. We'll find their fingerprints, trace them back to their hard drive, and infiltrate them."

"And the hit?" Sebastian asked, wanting details.

"Special treat of Emile's," Armando said, looking intently at Sebastian, who tried not to squirm under the man's heated gaze.

His stare was some mixture of undressing him and reaching into his soul. How could Armando be so blatant under Diego's watchful eye? And yet Diego seemed oblivious. He even pulled out his phone and began texting as if the topic of killing a woman bored him.

"We will wipe Daniela off the face of the earth," Emile said. "Your father will be happy. Now, let's talk about payment."

20

***

She was living a dream, and reality would come knocking soon, bursting this bubble. With the meals and games, she could almost let herself believe they were a family. But as each day passed, she felt the fallacy of her plan. There was no escaping the cartel. How had she ever deluded herself into thinking her life could be normal—whatever that was?

There would be no returning to WITSEC either. She'd burned that bridge by breaking their rules and running without informing them of the identity breach. She came to Rider SI for help but felt more like she'd brought a Trojan horse straight into the heart of the company. Jackson's work family.

She'd avoided Jackson for an entire day as she worked on her laptop and tried to ignore the guilt gnawing at her. After finishing a writing project and reading through it for errors, she submitted it to her editor. Next, she whisked through insurance claims, the much less rewarding job of the two she had.

After a foursome dinner of superficial pleasantries, she washed dishes as Jackson tidied the kitchen. Justin and Rafe left to the other room to play video games.

He wiped off the table with a rag. "All caught up on work?"

"Yes."

"It's good you can work remotely."

"Ah, yes. That was by design. I started working in an office for a small commercial rental company, keeping the books and maintaining the office. The pay was low, but so was the workload. Good for a woman with a young child." She loaded the dishwasher as she talked. "At night, I worked on college credits online, earning an associate's degree in business. When Justin started preschool, I sought remote work so I could get him to and from school every day."

"That's some hard work and initiative."

"I think part of me has always felt disconnected from society. An imposter. A black sheep in white wool. Remote work meant I didn't have to overplay my role as Celeste Rivera. Lastly, remote work meant I could move whenever I didn't feel safe or didn't like Justin's school."

"You had options."

"I had options."

When she finished loading and turned, Jackson was in front of her, drying his hands on the dish towel.

"Were you and Justin happy before Sebastian found you?"

She took the towel from him, fingers brushing, and dried her hands. "We were settled. We were as happy as we could be. Happy as a team." Many days she'd longed for the company of a man and a father figure for Justin.

"Remote work means you can disappear on me anytime, too. I feel like you've been putting distance between us today, Daniela. Intentional distance." The sadness in his voice tugged at her heart.

He was right, and distance wasn't fair to him. She dropped the towel on the dishwasher handle.

"You... you're all I've loved, Jackson. My whole life, you're the only man I've loved." Her tone held a wistful surrender rather than a happy confession. She hated that for him. A declaration of love should be a joyous occasion, not one overcast with dark clouds of fear and danger. "You're the only man I've ever been with."

His mouth fell open, and she moved to scrub a pan. If she kept her hands occupied and eyes on her task, maybe she could force out the words he needed to hear.

She continued, "You're perfect. *In my imagination*, you were off saving the world while we were apart. You are this flawless knight in shining armor. You can't live up to the pedestal I put you on. No man can. I've never felt safe with anyone except you, but you're not real." She placed the pan on the rack to drip and dried her hands on a kitchen towel again.

He took her shaking hand and placed it against his heart. "I'm real. I'm flawed. You bet your ass I'm flawed, but I love you. I'd be honored to spend the rest of my life showing you how real and flawed I am. Sometimes I'll upset you. Sometimes I'll down right piss you off. But I'll never betray you." He placed a finger under her chin and lifted her eyes to meet his. "And anytime I've hurt your feelings, I promise incredible make up sex."

She chuckled lightly as her heart softened. "You want this? An instant family?"

"More than anything." He lifted her hand to his mouth and kissed. "Justin can be the first of many."

Her lashes fluttered in surprise. "And all the baggage that comes with us?"

"The load isn't so heavy when you don't have to carry it alone."

She stepped into his arms, wrapped hers around him, and lost herself in another glorious kiss.

SEBASTIAN PULLED his shirt on and tucked it into his pants, not making eye contact with his lover. Sebastian had succumbed to his physical and emotional desires last night when Armando had sent an encrypted message to meet in a hotel room in Savannah. Nearing sunrise, rational thinking now prevailed. He needed to slip away before spying eyes found the pair of them together.

"I wish we could share more time together, not just in the shadows." Armando pulled the sheets to cover himself.

"That way lies death for us both."

"This is all we are, then?" Armando's voice was soft and sorrowful. "Living fake, unfulfilling lives, pretending to be something we aren't?"

Sebastian gave a bitter chuckle. "Doesn't that describe most people as they try to fit into the society of their upbringing?"

Armando looked away, which had Sebastian regretting how harsh he'd sounded. He brought his shoes over the edge of the bed and sat beside where Armando lay. "I don't want to see you get hurt."

Armando looked up at him hopefully, adoringly. "But my plan—"

"I heard your plan," Sebastian interrupted. He'd listened to Armando's scheming, which held some appeal. "It's a fantasy. A beautiful one. But it's too risky."

For both of their sakes, Armando would be *The Road Not Taken.*

Two roads diverged in a yellow wood,
And sorry I could not travel both
And be one traveler, long I stood
And looked down one as far as I could
To where it bent in the undergrowth

"Do you say that because you truly believe it, or you don't want to be with me?" Armando asked.

Sebastian gently gripped Armando's chin in his hand to hold eye contact. "If there were a way that didn't end in us both dying, I would choose you." He tugged on his shoes and walked toward the door.

"And your cousin?" Armando asked.

"She has three Horsemen left. The odds are stacked against her."

Mica arrived early the next morning at Bones, a car detail shop turned underground headquarters belonging to Rider SI. She took the secret entrance—an underground parking lot attendant booth with a hidden staircase leading to a tunnel to their hideout.

She entered, setting her coffee and keys down on a table. Claire sat at her desk, furiously typing. The tech guru didn't spare Mica a glance.

"We're under attack." Her strained voice squeaked out the words.

"What?" Mica jolted.

"We're being hacked. I'm working to identify the source and block them, but they still got in."

"How long have you been at this? Why didn't you message me?" Mica asked.

Fingers flying over the keyboard, Claire sniffed. "Sixty seconds. These aren't Script Kiddies. I'm battling professionals who were able to reach root access. I can't type hundreds of lines of code and alert you at the same time. They were ready for me. Last night, I powered down everything like I do each night and disconnected ethernet cables. As soon as everything was live this morning, and the computer was on, they pounced."

Mica stared at the screens. Dozens of open windows appeared to be mostly done and looked like gibberish. When Mica had been a bounty hunter, she'd taught herself the way around most low-tech computer software programs and how to steal information, including deleted files and search browser histories. Whatever Claire was up to looked far more complex, although it usually did.

Mica weighed the need for more information against distracting Claire. "What information did they get?"

"Their search terms were hunting for anything to do with Jackson or Daniela."

Daniela was simple—they hadn't created an official file. Her name wouldn't be in Rider data, but the company had plenty of information on Jackson.

Mica's heart rate kicked up a notch. "Can they find out he's staying at Reece's? Is that documented somewhere?"

Armando and Emile. This had to be the pair of Horsemen—one of which was a computer hacker—coming after Daniela for the bounty.

"They found Daniela." Claire never stopped typing.

"Dang it, Claire. I need to warn them." Mica whipped out her phone.

"They won't escape before the drone strikes."

"Did you say *drone*?" Mica's mouth went dry. Her whole body shuddered with fear that the family and Rafe were about to die. She pulled out her phone and dialed Jackson's number.

As it rang, she envisioned the stirring occupants at Reece's house. Daniela and Jackson would be drinking coffee, and Justin would be watching TV. Rafe was probably on the back porch, talking to Dia as he looked over the grassy lawn.

Meanwhile, a long, sleek, charcoal-colored UAV—unmanned aerial vehicle—armed with a Hellfire missile, or maybe Sidewinder, silently glided through the air on a voyage to kill them all.

JACKSON STOOD BEHIND THE COUNTER, making eggs to order. A pile of already cooked bacon sat off to one side on a plate. He slid a steaming mound of scrambled eggs with cheese in front of Justin, who was sitting at the counter and munching on a piece of bacon. Jackson turned and, cracking open three more eggs, set to work on Daniela's omelet. Rafe sat on the couch in the living room, playing The Beatles' "Love Me Do" on his harmonica.

Jackson and his family had had three wonderful days together of normalcy, and if he wasn't careful, he would start imagining this was his family reunited and forever sharing a life together. He'd pushed Daniela early, letting her know the future he wanted. Perhaps that hadn't been fair—pressing her to form a family with him while she was relying on him for protection. She might have agreed out of obligation. Or worse, out of fear he would abandon her if she didn't. He hoped that hadn't been how she'd interpreted the situation.

When the danger finally passed, he didn't want her unhappy in a life she hadn't chosen freely. When this was over, he'd make sure she wanted him one more time. Until then, he could show her glimpses into a happiness they could share.

"Justin, what do you say?" Daniela prompted.

"Oh. Thanks for the eggs."

"You're welcome."

Thankfully, the boy wasn't tacking on 'Mr. Hart' to his words anymore.

Jackson added cheese, onion, and green pepper to the omelet in the pan. "I was thinking we could take a drive north, maybe go for a hike today."

"Some time outside four walls sounds nice," she agreed.

"North Georgia has some amazing places to hike," he said.

Before he could elaborate further, his phone chimed with an incoming call. Glancing at the screen, he saw Mica's name. He hoped for good news even as his nerve endings crackled with worry at an early morning call. "Boss."

"Jackson. Get everyone out of the house now. Incoming drone. Armed."

He knew better than to take time to ask questions. Answers could come later.

He cut off the stove and pocketed his phone, saying, "We're leaving now. Everyone to the car." He kept his voice firm, commanding, but without the alarm and terror squeezing his chest at the word *armed drone*.

"Take nothing and go. Rafe?"

He'd stopped playing his harmonica. "I heard you."

The four of them raced toward the garage as Jackson pressed the button to turn on his engine. While Justin piled in, Daniela grabbed the duffel bag by the garage stairs and dragged it with her into the back passenger seat.

Her go bag, Jackson knew. She probably had a change of clothes and all of those prepaid credit cards stuffed in there. The same bag she'd had with her when she'd first shown up at Rider SI.

Crap. Had he even improved her situation in the slightest? She was right back to running for her life again.

Rafe slapped the button on the wall to open the garage door before careening around the truck and hopping into the passenger's seat. Jackson slid into the driver's seat, put the engine in drive, and sent it speeding forward while simultaneously strapping on his seatbelt.

"What's doing, Jackson?" Rafe asked.

"We're compromised. Mica said something about an attack drone."

"When will it strike?"

"I don't know." Jackson glanced in the rearview mirror as they left the house behind. His heart thudded as he wondered what the blast radius would be.

"How did they find us?" Rafe asked.

Jackson shot an irritable glance at his partner. "Don't know that either. Mica called and said get out of the house and we did. That's all the information I have."

Rafe opened up his phone and placed a call. After not getting an answer, he hung up.

"Armando," Rafe suggested. "He's the hacker Horseman. Maybe he traced someone's computer or phone."

Jackson's mouth went dry. He hoped that wasn't the case. They all had their phones on them, so if the drone targeted a phone and not Reece's house...

Game over.

After another minute passed, Jackson felt some of the tension ease out of his shoulders. He hadn't known what the drone was armed with, but they were now several miles out and safe from any explosion, if the house was the target.

"Where are we going?" Daniela asked.

"We'll find a new safe house."

"Mica didn't answer when I called." Rafe said.

"Maybe she's got her hands full."

21

___

"Уou get through my firewalls, assholes. I get through yours." Keystroke after keystroke, Claire worked furiously. Her gaze never left her monitors, and her mouth twisted in concentration. "There you are. Return to sender, bitch!"

Mica didn't remember a time when Claire cursed so vividly. Mica paced, counting the seconds and wondering if Jackson and Daniela were out of range yet.

When Claire opened other tabs, her screen changed from lines of code to a map of Savannah, and the image zoomed steadily to street level.

"You sent their attack drone back at them?" Mica asked, unable to conceal the mixture of horror and awe in her voice.

"Yes. I programmed it back to its starting coordinates."

"Okay. Do we know the type of weapon it has? Do we know the blast radius? We don't know the magnitude of the damage. There could be people around them."

Claire shook her head. "They're on a boat." She zoomed in on the map to reveal a marina. "I tracked their IP address."

"Okay. Maybe the damage will be contained."

Now that Mica could see Claire's face, she witnessed the strain around her eyes and the pale, glass-like fragility, suggesting she might crack at any moment.

A heavy weight settled in the air.

Mica placed a hand on her shoulder. "Is it over?" Without live cameras, she didn't know the status of the enemy.

Claire nodded as her shoulders sagged.

"You saved Jackson, Daniela, their son, and Rafe. You did good. Very good."

Claire lowered her head. "I sent their weapon back to them. I killed people with a bomb." Tears welled in her eyes.

"You saved a family, Claire. Can you investigate the damage done at the marina?"

Sullen, Claire nodded.

Mica sent a quick text to Drake, Claire's husband, asking him to come provide moral support. Next, she texted Jackson to let him know two more horsemen had fallen and he and his family should take refuge in a hotel for the night.

"THIS WAS A MISTAKE. Coming to you for help was a mistake. You could have been killed. Rafe could have been killed." Daniela paced the hotel room, frustration and fear bubbling through her, thick like a pit of tar.

They were registered under Rafe's name. He'd taken Justin down to swim in the hotel pool, and Daniela was grateful because she needed to pull herself together. She'd held Justin tight in the car and had given him reassurance, now she needed her own.

They'd been targeted by a bomb.

Capital B-O-M-B!

Jackson gave her space. Maybe he wasn't sure which version of her he would see—angry Daniela lashing out or doleful Daniela needing comfort. So far, he hadn't turned away from any of her moods.

"We're okay," he said. "We're all alive. If you and Justin were out there on your own, you'd both be dead. Because you're with me—with Rider—no one is dead. Except two more Horsemen."

"They are?" She looked up at him hopefully.

"Yes. Mica texted me. Claire destroyed them with their own bomb."

She lunged at him and wrapped her arms around him. "*Ah, dios. Only one left. One.*"

The most dangerous one, she suspected. But only one. She gauged how she felt about men dying so she could live. They had chosen their fate. She wouldn't lose sleep over them.

Jackson hugged her back.

She buried her face in his neck. "I've always felt safest right here, in your arms."

"You'll always be safe with me. Thank you for trusting me, for coming to me." He leaned her back, wiped at a tear on her cheek. "You've given me a wonderful gift these last few days with you and Justin."

"You make a wonderful father." She sniffed. "*Nosotros le diremos.* When this is over, we'll tell him everything. I hope he'll forgive me for lying. For telling him his father died in a house fire and all memorabilia was lost."

Jackson tilted his head to one side as he regarded her.

She shrugged. "I needed a reason why he would never see you again and why we had no pictures. And I didn't want him to blame you if I'd concocted a story about how you had to leave or we had to leave and have no contact whatsoever."

He rubbed gentle hands up and down her arms. "Makes sense. We'll tell him when the time is right."

She nodded, her heart gushing with adoration for this man as she stared up into his blue eyes. "I love you."

His mouth curved. "I'll never tire of hearing that. Maybe absence makes the heart grow fonder or maybe a person can fall in love in a week, but I'm pretty sure I've loved you since our first conversation." He pulled her into his arms.

Uno se quedó. Just one left, she thought.

SEBASTIAN SAT before his father again. Although he remained still, his stomach churned in turmoil—had been ever since he'd heard about the drone destroying Armando and Emile's boat. Under the table, his right hand trembled slightly. Nicotine withdrawal, he knew, but he'd dry heaved when he'd tried to smoke earlier today. Because of this, he'd avoided his *cigarillos* since the explosion.

"*Padre.* One horseman remains."

His father's face was pale. Was he ill? He had heart problems, but he took medication for that.

"You are well?" Sebastian said, interested to discern not the faintest concern in his own voice.

Hermes glared at him. "Of course, I'm well." His tone suggested Sebastian's inquiry implied he thought his father was showing weakness. "I'm wanting this issue resolved." He flexed his left hand, shook out the arm. His face grimaced slightly.

"I'm working on it." Sebastian had been working on it, traveling from Central and South America to New York and Savannah and back and forth visiting his father. He'd been mostly living out of a suitcase for the last ten days.

"If Diego doesn't finish this, you'll unleash the bees." Another order from his father.

Sebastian carried the electronic device to summon *Las Abejas.* He'd taken the small comfort of never having used the gismo since it had been in his possession.

"No," Sebastian said flatly. "I agreed to the Horsemen. Then this is over."

"If I didn't know better, I might suspect you were rooting for your cousin." A bead of sweat trickled down the side of Hermes's face.

"You killed her father." *You forced my one true friend into hiding,* Sebastian thought. He stood even though he hadn't been dismissed. "You've done enough to her. She deserves peace with her son." Maybe Daniela could win this and have the family and love of a man that Sebastian never could.

His father's face went red with fury, and, looking down at him, Sebastian found his anger didn't threaten him this time. Hermes' eyes turned calculating. He would certainly set Diego against Sebastian when he was done with Daniela, but Hermes underestimated his son, who had his own plan.

MICA WALKED around the zoo with David and Allen. They were bundled in light jackets, enjoying the fall breeze, which seemed to make the animals friskier. Her son was especially enthralled by the penguins.

"You okay?" David asked, taking her hand. He always sensed when she was distracted with work.

"Sorry." She tried to focus on her son's enjoyment of the animals. "I'm struggling to set aside all that's happened in the last twenty-four hours." According to local news reports in Savannah, the boat explosion had caused property damage and was suspected to have claimed the lives of two people who'd been on the destroyed yacht. Bodies among the wreckage had yet to be identified.

"Claire doesn't think the drone bomb can be traced back to the Rider team," Mica told David.

"But...?"

"But if the Feds recover any of the boat hardware, they might find evidence that the boat owners had been searching for the Rider team —specifically Jackson."

"You're worried the FBI will investigate your company."

"Yeah. I just hope the explosion rendered Armando and Emile's equipment unsalvageable."

"Then there's the immediate danger to Jackson and his family."

"Yes. The fourth and final Horseman remains."

What are you up to, Diego Aguilar?

When they reached the monkeys, David picked up Allen so he could have a better view. If David could put down his stressful ER work and enjoy family time, so could she. Smiling, she snuggled up to him to enjoy the rambunctious simians.

Mica's phone rang, and she withdrew it to see a number she didn't recognize. "Mica Rider."

"It's Nash. You said to call if I had a problem. I have a problem."

Technically, she'd told him to call if he needed help, and she suspected this was actually the nature of his call.

"I'm listening."

Golden lion tamarins swung back and forth on ropes, danced on their poles, and screamed at each other. She couldn't be certain if these were just expressions of life, aggressive, pre-mating tactics, or males getting ready to battle.

Not my circus, not my monkeys.

"The cartel has my niece. They're demanding I bring them Daniela César in exchange. I recognized the name of Alejandro César's daughter, the one who went into WITSEC after testifying against her uncle. But I told them I don't know where the fuck she is. They told me Jackson Hart knows exactly where she is. So, I don't know what kind of illegal shit you're wading in, but we need to talk about how we're getting my niece back."

Mica used two fingers to rub her temple. *My circus, my monkeys.* And the big top was about to come crashing down around all—on top of all of them.

22

───────

*D*aniela found herself once again in the conference room inside Rider headquarters. Jackson was by her side, though stoic. Mica sat near the head of the table by the big screen mounted on the wall and Claire was across from her. Justin was safely back at the hotel with Rafe. Other Rider team members she didn't recognize had joined via video conference call.

"Here's the situation," Mica began. "Six years ago, Daniela César witnessed the death of her father. His brother shot Alejandro César in cold blood. Daniela testified against Hermes César, and he went to prison. Eleven days ago, Daniela and her son were found by the Colombian cartel, despite being in the Witness Protection Program. She came to us for help. Daniela and Jackson met with Sebastian César, Hermes' son and proctor, and Diego Aguilar, one of the cartel's deadliest men in power." She paused for a sip of water.

Daniela suspected the summary was for the benefit of other Rider team members to fully understand the situation.

Mica continued, "The cartel promised to send four assassins after Daniela. They also promised that this would be the last of their efforts to eliminate her, meaning that if she survives the Four Horsemen, she would no longer be a target. Three horsemen are down."

Mica stood and paced. "On the call with us today is DEA agent Nash Rucker. He and his teammates have been working to undermine the Colombian cartel, but the cartel discovered a link between Nash's partner and Jackson. And Jackson and Daniela. The cartel kidnapped Nash's niece and are demanding an exchange of Daniela for his niece. Nash has agreed to take part in this meeting and listen to our plan with his caveat that if he doesn't like our plan, he will implement his own."

Daniela's mind reeled. Kidnapping a girl? That was so far from anything she thought Sebastian was capable of executing. There must be nothing left of the cousin she'd loved.

She glanced at the screen, focusing on a tanned, rugged looking man in his early thirties with a square jaw and keen eyes. He was staring at the monitor, and the word 'Nash' was listed beneath his video image.

Her whole body tensed at the thought of a DEA agent staring at her. The US government officials had taken away everything from her under the guise of keeping her safe. A chill crept up her spine at the memory of her hopelessness six years ago when she'd turned her life over to them.

A warm hand slipped into hers, grounding her. When she looked at Jackson, he gave her a gentle smile.

"Nash is in law enforcement. Why isn't he running an op through the DEA or FBI?" Reece asked.

Mica looked at Reece on the screen. "Mr. Rucker is currently on suspension pending an investigation of the death of an agent. In an event unrelated to this, he uncovered one of their own taking a cut. His options were kill or be killed."

Silence settled as everyone seemed to digest that bit of information.

"We have to make the exchange," Daniela said.

All eyes whipped toward her.

"I mean, obviously, I don't go with the cartel." She shifted her weight in her chair. "That's the part where Rider security ensures my safety. But to get the girl back, I'll have to make an appearance. I won't be responsible for the death of this man's niece."

Still silence. Jackson was rigid as a stone.

"We go," she continued. "To my cousin, it appears we're complying. In the background, Rider does what Rider does, right?" Was the room growing hotter? "You're the Rider team. You've already stopped three of the Four Horsemen. You saved rockstar Ethan Storm. You saved billionaire weapons developer Bill Sharp's daughter. You saved a country's First Lady and family."

The silence drew out as Daniela reflected on her own words. Was she trying to convince them to help or convince herself they were the right team for the job? *Ah dios*, she didn't want to put lives at stake, but she couldn't do this without them.

Nash continued to stare intently at her, almost squinting through the camera like he wanted a better view.

Daniela felt forced to break the quiet again. "I'm sorry your niece was kidnapped because of a feud the Colombian cartel has with me. I will go. I'll help you get her back."

"Unfortunately," Mica said, "I agree with you, and I don't see any other way to navigate this situation without pretending to offer you up on a platter. That leaves the question of how to present you. Does Nash appear to go rogue and kidnap you for the sake of rescuing his family?" She glanced at him. "He certainly has anger management issues to suggest he's capable of such a thing, so kudos to him for giving us a chance first."

On the screen, Nash bristled but didn't speak.

Mica continued, "Or would they believe Daniela, being who she is, willingly accompanies Nash because she can't stomach the thought of a terrified little girl somewhere held hostage by drug dealers and pond scum?"

"Sebastian knows I would come," Daniela said with resignation. "He would believe I would come willingly for the life of a child. But he would know I wouldn't come alone and wouldn't be taken without a fight."

Mica nodded. "Then that's the play. As Daniela pointed out, we have a lot of successes under our belts… some of which is public knowledge. The cartel hacked our computer system, which means they know not only Jackson Hart is protecting Daniela but so is the full force of the Rider team. We'll need everyone not on assignment and a few people we haven't worked with before."

She looked directly at Nash on the screen. "I'm sure our DEA agent has already begun reaching out to his loyalist, shadiest colleagues to see who is willing to help—off the record—to rescue a little girl."

Nash's eyes went wide on the screen, and he didn't deny it.

"I'm with Daniela," Jackson said.

"Here's my issue with that," Mica began as if she'd expected this part of the conversation. "The cartel found you because of a romantic interlude years ago. They know Daniela came to you for safety. At this point, they probably suspect a relationship between you two. If you accompany Daniela and Nash, the cartel won't believe you would allow for the exchange of Daniela for Nash's niece. Daniela must be there. Nash must pick up his niece. The cartel will see no use for you other than interference, and you'll be shot on site."

Jackson frowned but didn't disagree.

Mica continued, "You'll be there. Just not with Daniela. Everyone has twenty-four hours to get to Texas and prepare. We'll go over the schematics of the location next. After that, we break for travel. Bill Sharp has agreed to loan us his private jet—again—to travel there."

Daniela took in the team around her and on the screen. Supportive expressions surrounded her. She was grateful and determined to somehow pay them back in some small measure. When this was over, she would have to think of a way to express her gratitude.

Word of the day: imperilment. The state of not being protected from injury, harm, or peril. Traveling into the spider's web was to the imperilment of Daniela. Jackson focused on Claire's details, even as he hated how this plan didn't have him by Daniela's side.

They would meet at an abandoned town in southern Texas.

According to Claire, it had been a small but bustling railroad stop forced to desertion from economic hardships and lack of water. The town became one of a dozen ghost towns in Texas for similar reasons.

The satellite images revealed a cantina of crumbling limestone walls around a large courtyard. The rectangular area had probably once been a lovely garden with winding paths but was now overgrown with weeds and tangled bushes. Opposite of that were storefronts for a hotel, bar, post office, and country store. Jackson wondered if any of the roofs would be stable enough for a sniper to lurk in hiding. Still, the walls themselves could conceal a few dozen men.

Trap! Jackson's mind screamed. But they had no choice. One horseman stood between Daniela and her freedom. Between Jackson and having his family as a cohesive unit. Every scenario he played in his mind had this ending in bloodshed. Whose was yet to be determined.

"We'll fly a drone over the town immediately before the meet while it's still dark to get heat signatures," Claire said.

"Which means," Mica interjected, "we can tell you how many cartel men are there but not their exact location since it won't be real time."

Red arrows appeared on the slide show, indicating the entry and exit points as Mica continued, "Daniela and Nash will go through the west entrance. Rafe, Jackson, and Reece will lead Nash's volunteers to flank the sides at these entry points. Two teams. Two points of entry."

"The land is flat. The cartel will see the vehicles coming for miles," Jackson said.

"You won't arrive by land," Mica said. "We'll parachute the team in under cover of darkness before dawn."

"Won't the cartel hear the planes?" Daniela asked.

There was no avoiding some low, distant noise. Rafe had told him about Bill Sharp's silent, electric aircraft, but it wasn't large enough to hold a team of men.

"One plane, and it won't buzz low," Nash said, who was apparently now on board with the plan. "You'll use black parachutes, and we'll have the LZ a mile out. You'll have to hump from the landing zone to the facility in full gear and chutes before sunrise."

"What do we do about mitigating casualties?" Reece asked. "This could turn into a bloodbath on US soil. No way to use those nanoparticles out in the open."

Jackson agreed. Rider was about security and protection. They weren't killers.

"Claire worked with Jess and Jenna on tranquilizer guns." Mica held up a hand when murmurs of protest started in the group. "They won't replace your guns, but they carry six rounds and are good for close range."

She held up a black pistol, smaller than Jackson would have expected for a tranq gun. "Obviously, if your attacker is drawing a weapon on you, you'll need to use your gun, not a sedative. The injection takes from one to five minutes for full effect, and a lot can happen in a fight during that time. But this is a sneak attack, so you will catch some men by stealth, and this is the gun to use. Claire will send full specs on the weapon with the rest of the mission details. You will all also get pepper spray and tear gas."

She set the weapon down on the tabletop. "Subdue, restrain, and move on until every cartel man is on the ground in twist ties. Lethal ammunition when it's your life or theirs. We get the girl, and we get our people out. When we're clear, Claire will get an anonymous tip to the FBI for them to claim Diego and anyone else from their most wanted list."

Jackson rubbed his neck as he absorbed the scheming and expense Mica had gone through to set up the rescue. Despite careful planning, any number of things could go wrong... including the very real possibility of him losing Daniela.

23

*D*aniela held tight to Justin as Jackson finished loading the vehicle. Jackson had already hugged Justin goodbye before leaving mother and son alone in the living room. Mica waited outside, speaking with Rafe. Daniela was leaving Justin behind with Mica again as she took another flight to meet with her cousin.

"You'll stay with Mica again," she said, half choking on the words to hold back a sob. She needed to be strong for him.

"They're cool," Justin said.

She pulled back, looked her son in the eyes. "This trip may be a few days, like the last one." She wouldn't talk about what ifs, but in case she didn't make it back alive, she'd written Justin a letter, which she had given to Mica.

Daniela prayed her son never had to open it.

"But you'll have Jackson with you, so it will be okay, like last time," Justin said, tone suggesting he'd detected the gravity of this trip even though she'd avoided giving him details.

Daniela smiled. "Yes, you're right."

In and out like last time.

She hugged him again tightly, probably too tight, but she sought to ease the squeezing sensation in her chest.

She would face her cousin again. Unlike the church, this time she would be armed. They would make the exchange for Nash's niece and incapacitate Diego so that the DEA agent and his men could arrange an arrest.

Her only job was to stay alive until the cavalry arrived.

DANIELA STEPPED inside the hotel room with the two queen beds and surveyed the layout. Jackson followed behind her, wheeling in the luggage she knew contained bullet-resistant clothing and guns. Tomorrow would be her end or a new beginning.

She didn't want to think about that now.

He said, "I know it's one room, but I'd feel better if we shared. I'm worried the cartel could have people watching the hotels within a fifty-mile radius of the meet, intending to find you before tomorrow."

"I like sharing a room with you." She fully intended to make the most of it. She pulled the thick curtains closed, kicked off her shoes, and let her hair down out of its clip.

Jackson set up one bag on the luggage rack in the closet, still talking as he worked. "I'll leave here at midnight to go to the airstrip, but you have Nash's number, and he's just down the hall if you need anything before the two of you head out in the morning."

She pulled her shirt off over her head and dropped it to the floor.

Jackson was bent over the baggage, rummaging through it. He pulled out a toiletries bag and walked into the bathroom as he continued talking. "I asked some old contacts about Nash. Nobody likes his personality, but they say he's trustworthy. He's not part of the Rider team, and he has a bit of a temper, but overall, I'm sensing he'll keep his word to protect you. If I didn't, I wouldn't have agreed to let you go with him."

She shimmied out of her jeans and kicked them aside.

The sink ran for just a moment, followed by a brushing noise. "Are you okay?" Jackson stepped out of the bathroom, toothbrush in hand, and blinked at her, having not noticed she'd been undressing the entire time he'd been talking.

She chuckled at his surprise, liking how she could shock and surprise the unflappable Jackson Hart.

She finished undressing altogether. "I'm not wasting these next precious hours we have before you leave."

"Hold that thought." He disappeared back into the bathroom and reemerged empty-handed. "You take my breath away, Daniela." He unbuttoned his shirt. "All I have to do is look at you and I'm lost. And also somehow found."

She stepped toward him, pressed her lips to his bare chest. So firm, so warm. His hungry gaze had her feeling powerful and vulnerable at the same time. He placed a hand under her chin and tilted her head so their eyes met.

Jackson Hart.

The man who had her heart.

"I want you, Daniela. I'm looking forward to a future with you."

"It's hard to think about a future together when I don't know if there's a tomorrow." She shuddered.

He wrapped warm arms around her, and she let herself melt against him. "There will be a tomorrow and many more after that. I want them all with you. You and Justin." He drew back, looking at her with a bottomless depth of compassion and longing. "I love you, Daniela."

She smiled and drew him against her. "When Justin was young, my father was still alive. I didn't trust anyone who would work for him. Then, in WITSEC, I wasn't willing to risk getting close to anyone. Intimacy required a level of trust I couldn't afford for Justin's safety. But I trust you. I trust a future with you."

Eyes glittering with affection, he leaned down and pressed his mouth to hers. The kiss was richly deep, a promise to cherish the trust she'd put in him.

His hands roamed her body, sending sparks of tantalizing desire coursing along her skin before coalescing and plunging to her core.

Still kissing and caressing, he took her down to the bed, though he left her panting for a moment as he finished undressing.

Then, he was over her, naked, with muscles taut and eyes a smoky blue. She ran fingers through his hair while he pressed kisses to her neck. Lips tantalized her breast as his fingers explored lower. Within moments, her body was writhing with need for him.

She urged him up and into her, arching to meet his initial thrust, moaning as she tugged him down closer and wriggled her legs around him. "I want a future with you."

"You'll have it. I love you." He drew back and thrust.

Each time felt deeper, more sublime. They fell into a rhythm, drawing out the delicious friction.

"Look at me, Daniela."

Their eyes met as the last thrust pushed her to the edge and over. He took the plunge with her, rocking steadily until he collapsed onto her.

DARKNESS HAD SETTLED OUTSIDE, and midnight grew nearer. Jackson was relaxed in bed after lovemaking. Daniela's warm, silky skin caressed his where her limbs entwined around him. Part of him wanted to preserve this sublime moment forever, and part of him wanted the clock to tick faster. The sooner they pushed past their confrontation with the cartel, the sooner his life with Daniela could begin.

Word of the day: exigent. Things that need to be dealt with immediately.

Daniela's predicament and the kidnapping of Nash's niece had created exigent circumstances.

She pressed her lips to his bare chest. "This is the part where you tell me the entire mission will be a breeze. That you eat danger for breakfast. That your team could take on the cartel in their sleep."

His stomach knotted. "I won't lie to you, Daniela. This is dangerous as hell. I've never been in as much danger in my years at the FBI as I am regularly with Rider SI. This isn't an action movie where the hero has a decade of hard living and dead bodies in his past to attest to his superior capability. But I can promise you, I don't go down easy. And I will be between you and any danger that comes our way."

She kissed his bare chest again. Despite their leisurely naked lounging, events were moving quickly as they plunged headlong into danger.

"The Rider team is damn good at what they do. I can't guarantee the outcome, but I can guarantee that this team gives us the best chances of winning."

She snuggled closer with a smile and a shake of her head. "Honest to a fault."

"I'll protect you." His voice held unwavering conviction.

He wouldn't be by her side the entire time like he preferred, but he would get to her and keep Diego from claiming the bounty... and her life.

Jackson didn't like free-falling. His emotions transitioned from a flipping stomach knotted with fear to the sensation of plummeting through a bottomless dream to acceptance that he would absolutely die to a calm peace in the black night sky.

Parachuting wasn't an activity required to work for the FBI, and he'd never been a daredevil. However, with the open layout of the abandoned town, dropping in was the only viable sneak attack. Nash was friends with a jump instructor and pilot who'd been willing to take up the crew on short notice and fly them over the abandoned town. Jackson had received a twenty-minute crash course on how to survive while on the airplane with Reece, Ryan, Rafe, and a handful of Nash's agent buddies.

Now, he blinked at his lighted altimeter, which dizzily spiraled. He wasn't sure if seeing the ground rushing toward him would've been any more reassuring than the black pit below him.

At three thousand feet, he pulled his cord. His body jerked like a puppet on the strings of a marionette. His stomach lurched in another protest. He kept his eyes on the altimeter to be prepared next for touchdown. He wasn't any good to Daniela if he blew out a knee on the landing.

On impact with the ground, his body jarred. He tumbled, tangling in the strings that ran from the harness to the parachute. Fortunately, a landing in darkness meant no one else witnessed the lack of grace with which he now attempted to detangle himself like a fly from a web.

The thrill of having survived and the adrenaline of needing to get to the town to be in position when Daniela arrived were the only things keeping his dinner in his stomach as opposed to the dirt floor.

By the time he rolled his shute and wriggled his earpiece in place, others had joined him. Together, they covered their gear beneath a camouflage tarp to be retrieved at a later time. Dressed in camo fatigues and Kevlar vests, the eight men jogged toward the ghost town under cover of darkness.

They kept communication chatter to a minimum. Jackson felt the weight of everything packed in his eight cargo pockets—a 9mm, Claire's specialized tranquilizer gun, a couple of protein bars, a camel pack of water with a straw looped around for easy access, and a trauma bandage with a few other first aid supplies.

"Mica's drone has done his flyby," Reece said to everyone. "There's a barn-like structure on the north side of town. It's empty. We'll converge there. Sunrise in forty-five minutes."

Showdown in forty-five minutes, Jackson thought.

Right now, Daniela was in Nash's custody, driving toward this destination. Jackson hated that he couldn't be with her, but Mica's reasoning was sound. He couldn't come up with a logical explanation to justify his presence by her side—one that wouldn't have him shot on site. Dead, he was no good to Daniela.

By the time Jackson reached the barn, Reece and Rafe had already swept the premises to ensure it was unoccupied. Everyone shuffled inside. Jackson was pouring sweat and his legs burned, but he had a few minutes of downtime before sunrise. Before he needed to reach Daniela.

When he heard her voice in his earpiece, he would know it was time to move. Of course, best laid plans and all... if the cartel had any tech to block transmissions, they could end up radio silent. In that case, they had a plan to move building by building and clear out any threats.

24

Heart thudding and nerves pinging with dread, Daniela stood beside Nash and took in her surroundings. The weather in September in southern Texas was warm with a faint humidity in the air, reminding her just how close they stood to the Mexican border and the Gulf Coast. The meet was a rundown old town with half dead vines creeping up the crumbling limestone walls and warped pale wood. Overgrown brush sprouted at the bases of buildings, surviving but not thriving. The air was so quiet as she faced the town, she half expected a tumbleweed to roll by, followed by a twang of Texas showdown music.

Out there somewhere was Jackson Hart and Mica's team, working with a few of Nash's friends to surround and secure this place. She glanced at Nash, the DEA agent she was putting far too much trust in. No. Her trust was in Jackson, who had told her to trust Nash. Her trust was in Mica, who agreed to have Nash and his team on this mission.

"I'm grateful for you taking this risk and helping my niece," Nash said.

"I didn't have a choice," Daniela said.

"You did. You could have chosen not to risk your life for a little girl you don't even know. You had a choice, and I'm grateful. You chose to be the hero."

"You're welcome." The author in her wanted to correct his gender choice of the noun hero, but she understood he was trying to ease the tension between them, and now was not the time for corrections.

"I didn't get off on the right foot with the Rider team, and I'm sorry for that."

She glanced at him, seeing regret and worry etched on his tan face.

"I'm sorry your hostility resulted in the first time my son pulled the trigger of a gun." Her tone was sharper than intended, but she'd spoken a truth she wanted him to feel.

"I'm sorry for that, too. My behavior was inexcusable. I'll make amends for all of that today. We're all walking away from whatever happens here." His voice held an inspiring sort of conviction.

"You're risking your career, aren't you? Going outside the law to rescue your niece?"

"My career is already shot to hell," he said the words with hard acceptance.

"So, just your life, then?" she asked with light mocking.

He grunted. "Yeah, just that. But that's what we do for family."

"You had a choice," she said his words back to him. "You chose to be the hero."

"Yeah, okay." He smirked and rolled his shoulders as he seemed to acknowledge her point, despite the adjective making him uncomfortable. "Let's go be a couple of damn heroes."

As they approached the town, she felt the weight of the gun at her back beneath Mica's navy blazer she wore—bullet-resistant again, like something out of a *John Wick* movie. Daniela didn't want to get shot today. But what if she had to shoot someone else? What if she had to shoot Sebastian? Her once beloved cousin?

Yes, she would pull the trigger on him and those childhood memories if it meant keeping her family safe. Only if he posed a threat. She didn't want to hurt her cousin, and the agreement was her survival against the Four Horsemen. Sebastian wasn't one of them.

Diego Aguilar was. If Sebastian was hurt, Hermes could use his son's injury as an insult and re-initiate the bounty on Daniela's head. The complexities of the situation were mind-boggling.

Two men dressed in khaki cargo pants and T-shirts carried Ingram MAC pistols as they stepped out from behind alleyways. Daniela tried not to flinch. She recalled her father's men liking the submachine gun for how fast it could unload thirty rounds into its victim.

"Steady, Daniela." Nash's hushed voice was rough, but with a dose of bravado like a coach's encouragement. "If needed, I'll take care of Diego." He said the words as if he knew she was thinking of the demonic Horseman.

Jackson had explained to her that Nash's partner had identified Diego as the one who'd beaten her. He suspected he'd also snatched his niece. Daniela wasn't thrilled with the rage seething off Nash like heat off the desert sand, but if he directed his rage against her enemies, she could support it.

Her legs felt like lead, but she picked them up and moved forward. Any one of the cartel's men could fire at any moment. A head shot and her life was over. No, only Diego was allowed to fill that role. He wanted the payout. She had to cling to that agreement, at least.

One gunman moved his hand aside and held up his phone. He looked back-and-forth at Daniela and his screen, confirming this was the woman allowed in the town. Smart move, she thought. Nash could have used an undercover decoy to infiltrate this location.

"*Vamos.*" The guard pocketed his phone and motioned them forward.

She glanced at Nash, realizing the cartel men hadn't frisked their captives. She had entirely expected to be stripped of her weapon before meeting Diego and her untimely death.

The gunmen assumed positions, one in front and one behind, as they led Daniela and Nash down the dusty town lane. They turned and stepped up rickety stairs, onto a creaking wooden porch, and through rusted swinging doors. Her eyes adjusted to the dim light of a western bar, aged but still feeling frozen in time with a long, flat counter in front of empty shelves where she could easily visualize golden brown bottles of liquor. A dust-covered piano rested in one corner and a cobweb-laden poker table in another. The remainder of the floor was vacant. Stairs off to one side led to rooms on the second floor.

Sebastian leaned on the counter across from Diego and sipped whiskey in a shot glass beside a bottle, both of which looked too new to belong in this place. "Daniela," Sebastian said and had the gall to smile. His eyes held a glint of sadness at her stiff reaction as he straightened. He took a drag off the cigarette dangling carelessly between long fingers before dusting off his black three-piece suit, which had not a speck of lint on it.

"You look well, cousin. Handsome as ever," she said.

That earned her a warmer smile, one that looked reminiscent of his youth.

"It fits, right?" He spun in a circle, showing off his Pat Garret look, complete with boots, spurs, and a gleaming silver watch piece. He was only missing the mustache. "Once I picked this location—a classic for a showdown—I had to dress the part."

"You pull it off amazingly." Her voice was sincere. Whatever happened next, she could be civil and honest to the man who was once a treasured family member. "And meeting at the saloon is a nice touch." She'd watched enough American Western movies to know some wicked confrontations happened in saloons.

Diego grunted.

Sebastian tossed him an eye roll. "Diego does not approve of my choice of venue."

Exposed.

The word had first popped into Daniela's mind when Claire had shown the layout. This was no locked down compound like so many of the cartel's facilities. Mica's team could fan out and cover a dozen entry and exit points in the town.

Why had Sebastian chosen such an exposed little town when he surely had better options? Had he underestimated the number of

Rider employees and Nash's friends who could be rallied on short notice?

"My niece?" Nash said, breaking the silence.

"Ah, ah," Sebastian chided. "First, we frisk. Diego will be most angry with me if I don't remove weapons before I let our men lead you to your family."

When Sebastian moved forward, his two men raised their weapons, one pointed at Daniela and the other one at Nash. Nash's jaw ticked, and Daniela hoped he wouldn't do something foolish and hot-headed to get them both instantly killed.

Sebastian held out his hand to Daniela. Taking it meant moving several steps forward and away from Nash, which she was sure was Sebastian's intention. She accepted, and her hand landed in his. He raised it to his lips and kissed the back gently, his expression again oddly soft.

"I'm heart-broken you would kidnap a little girl," Daniela told Sebastian. "It's the work of a coward."

"You can take issue about that with Diego." Sebastian's tone suggested he hadn't approved of the abduction and easily deflected her insult onto the Horseman as if he agreed with her.

Sebastian dropped her hand, sidestepped, and approached Nash. His expression morphed into some mix of consternation and disdain. Patting him down, he removed the gun in the holster, but not the one at his ankle.

Had he not felt it? Daniela wondered. But his hands had glided over Nash's lower leg. Nash's expression betrayed nothing.

Sebastian moved back, set aside Nash's gun, straightened, and turned to Daniela. His hands moved over her, bumping into the tranquilizer gun at her back. His hands slid down into her coat pocket where he withdrew her Beretta 418.

He smiled broadly. "Yes, the Daniela I grew up with would be armed." He inspected the small weapon. "Not so changed, perhaps." He set the weapon on the windowsill.

Her mouth opened, but no words came out. He was letting her keep one gun while making everyone else think she was unarmed.

Her mind stuttered, trying to understand the situation Sebastian had orchestrated.

He glanced back at Diego and smirked. "Such a tiny weapon, though. You were right. She's a woman counting on men to save her. Just like my father suspected."

The cartel men snickered, and Daniela bristled. Sebastian's slight smile told her she'd given him the reaction he was hoping for.

He waved his hand. "Please escort Mr. Nash to his niece's holding room. They are allowed to leave unharmed, as per our agreement. He has delivered Daniela."

The two gunmen led the way, one in front and one behind Nash. He disappeared behind the squeaking barroom doors. She hadn't decided if she liked Nash or not, being a simultaneously hard and cracked sort of character, like chipped granite, but she felt alone without him.

"Now"—Sebastian leaned back on the bar and took another sip of his whiskey—"Diego tells me he is concerned that you may have brought Jackson Hart with you along with Rider team members, who may very well be surrounding us at this moment." Sebastian cocked his head to one side.

She said nothing. That was exactly what was happening.

"Obviously, I explained to Diego, given his concerns, that he couldn't outright kill you, because we may need you as a hostage in order to escape."

"Let me go free," Daniela said, bordering on exasperation. Sebastian was playing a game she didn't understand. "We end the feud now, with no more bloodshed."

"Alas." He gave a melodramatic sigh. "I am bound by my father's wishes."

A third cartel man stepped through the bar doors wearing a white suit and electric blue shirt. He brandished a 9mm in one hand, pointed down but his finger on the trigger. His glacier blue eyes held a sharp determination.

When she recognized him by Rider's files as one of the presumed dead Horsemen, Daniela froze with fear.

25

$\mathcal{A}$drenaline fueled Jackson's steps and heightened his awareness of the dark world around him. Sight and hearing sharpened.

All of his focus was on the conversation between Daniela and Nash. He was apologizing for his behavior in front of Daniela's son the other day. For now, the conversation was clear, but when the shooting started, Jackson would have a hard time hearing everything.

On Reece's command, the Rider team moved in conjunction with Nash's DEA friends in total silence, launching their attack using hand signals in the dim light. They converged at a blacksmith workshop.

On Ryan's signal, Reece set a tiny explosive device before moving a few feet to the side of the main door. When a quick pop of smoke released, Ryan moved in first, with Jackson on his heels.

Subdue and move on. Get to Daniela.

Reece and Ryan took aim, striking the surprised men with the tranquilizer darts. The medication would take a moment to kick in, but before the cartel's men could raise their weapons, Jackson, Rafe, and the DEA agents pounced.

Jackson clocked his target squarely on the jaw and felt a satisfactory crunch. When he didn't go down, Jackson delivered a second punch to the gut, followed by a blow to the back. Now face down on the dirt floor, Jackson hurried to secure the man's arms behind his back with flex ties.

Wiping sweat from his brow with the back of his hand, Jackson surveyed the room. Everyone had been subdued.

And almost everyone was right here in this room. The number of cartel men matched the total heat signatures from the earlier drone minus nine—Sebastian, Diego, Nash's niece, and six unknowns. The conglomeration in this room didn't sit right with Jackson because it was poor planning on the cartel's part.

Reece gave him the nod that he was free to go in pursuit of Daniela. Rafe followed on his heels, and Jackson's gaze darted left and right, ready for any threats to emerge, but none did.

Aside from the panting of some men who were probably finishing tying up the men in the barn, Jackson heard Daniela greet Sebastian and identify her location.

The saloon.

As he zig-zagged through, alert for danger, he thought back to everything from the start of Daniela's predicament. Diego had been the one to torture information out of the US Marshal and find Daniela's location. Sebastian had been the blunder at her house, where she'd had time to flee and find help. Sebastian had been the one to agree to meet peaceably at the church. Diego had been the one to undermine him and try to capture them. Sebastian had orchestrated the Four Horsemen to come after Daniela, but they'd been able to dispatch three of them easily. Diego had been the one to torture Nash's partner and had kidnapped Nash's niece, but Sebastian had arranged a meeting at an unprotected territory with many of his armed men in a single location for easy round up. The pattern suggested Sebastian may be helping them within the confines of the cartel.

"I have my niece," Nash said into the group comms. "Two men are down and restrained at the bank."

Jackson had to reach her before Diego, the fourth and final Horseman, unleashed his wrath.

"ARMANDO, WHAT ARE YOU DOING?" Sebastian demanded, heart leaping into his throat. How had he found him? Right. The hacker had probably tracked Sebastian's phone.

Armando's gaze cut over to him. Some mixture of sadness and resolve swirled in those beautiful eyes. "You know what I'm doing."

Sebastian knew. Armando had laid out his plan after their night together. He had agreed to Armando programming the strike drone with the routing system back to Emile's yacht, available for Claire to finagle. In one swoop, the Rider team had sent the drone back to the docks, eliminated Emile, created the assumption of Armando's death, and reduced the threat to Daniela down to one Horseman.

When Sebastian had first conceived the idea of a finite danger to Daniela, he'd had the barest of hope for her. With Armando's help, the tide had turned.

Armando had helped both him and Daniela, for which Sebastian was grateful, but he had rejected Armando's plans to kill Diego. That had been more of a risk than Sebastian was willing to take.

Here and now might present the perfect opportunity. The only witness would be Daniela. Sebastian needed only to convince her to say he and Armando had died in a showdown with Diego. Except, if she was implicated in Sebastian's death, Hermes would have another reason for recourse. Armando probably hadn't considered that.

Then there was the issue of bodies. The other part of Armando's plan was to bomb this place after they evacuated so authorities wouldn't be able to discern how many bodies were here and to whom they belonged.

"It still won't work," Sebastian tried to reason with him now, as he had the other night.

Armando raised the gun and pulled the trigger, but Diego must have suspected he was the target because he was already bolting over the bar. As the fourth Horseman disappeared in a crash on the floor, Sebastian was unsure if he'd been hit or not.

Movement in Sebastian's peripheral vision had him jerking his head in time to see Daniela had pulled out her gun. When she pulled the trigger, Armando jerked back.

No, no, no.

Sebastian had left Daniela armed to shoot Diego, not Armando.

"*Oh, Dios!*" Sebastian caught Armando as he fell backward, gun falling to the floor.

"Your father," Armando began, voice weak and brittle, "he died of a heart attack thirty minutes ago."

Had he? Sebastian had set his phone on do not disturb. How did Armando know? Ah, the hacker had probably cloned Sebastian's phone at some point. Sebastian ran a hand delicately through Armando's hair. The news of his father's death must have spurred Armando into action, carrying out his dangerous plans.

Hot tears seared Sebastian's cheeks as Armando's eyes drifted closed. Sebastian's heart—the one he'd thought had petrified long ago—shattered.

"What have I done?" Sebastian lamented, feeling lost in the woods on a snowy evening...

> *The woods are lovely, dark, and deep,*
> *But I have promises to keep,*
> *And miles to go before I sleep,*
> *And miles to go before I sleep.*

DANIELA'S MIND sputtered to catch up with events as she lowered the tranquilizer gun she'd just fired. Armando, whom Sebastian was now clutching like a lost lover, had shot Diego.

She hadn't wanted to take a chance that Armando, the third and *not* dead Horseman, was planning to shoot her next to take the reward money. But now she wondered if Armando had shot Diego for Sebastian and not for his own financial ambitions.

Her heart melted for a moment to think Sebastian might have found somebody in the chaotic, brutal, homophobic world of the cartel.

"*Es una pistola tranquilizante*," she told him. "He's just sleeping. I don't... I don't actually know how long the sedative lasts. I can ask Jackson as soon as he gets here."

Sebastian looked at her with distant eyes, blinking several times as her words seemed to seep into his brain.

"Not lethal?"

"No." She gave him a soft smile as she stepped forward and bent toward him.

A roar erupted from behind the bar, where Diego staggered to his feet.

Daniela jerked upright.

He was bleeding from—somewhere. Red streaks smeared his face, perhaps from Armando's bullet or perhaps from smashing into the glass on the back wall. Blood stained his shirt over his left shoulder and dripped down his bare arm. He looked around wildly, blinking. Wiping his eyes, he stumbled around to maneuver out from behind the bar as he raised Pepe and took aim at Daniela.

Tranquilizer gun still in hand, Daniela fired first at Diego. She was aiming for his neck where the V of his jacket left skin exposed, but the strike hit lower. She knew from the debriefing with Claire and Mica that the needle wouldn't penetrate the thick leather, so the medication would never be effectively delivered.

She'd lost.

She'd taken a gamble that she could earn her freedom. Justin's freedom. But the price for failure was death. Maybe she should have taken her chances and gone back into WITSEC. She would never know if that had been the safer option.

Diego, momentarily distracted by the wasted dart, took aim again, face contorting with a wicked, self-satisfied smile.

He glanced at Sebastian. "I knew you were a disgrace to your father. I'll take the bounty on Daniela, and then I'll deal with you."

But before Diego could pull the trigger, gunshots pierced the window in front of the saloon. Diego flinched and the bullet from his gun flew wide when he squeezed the trigger.

A split second later, Jackson crashed through the glass directly into Diego.

Daniela crouched to avoid the flying shards. When she looked up, the men were pummeling each other with fists, knees, and elbows. Diego looked like a red demon with blood spatter on his face and hands as he snarled and battled. Dirt covered Jackson, as if he'd already fought some hard won hand-to-hand battles.

Daniela eased closer to get a shot into Diego and saw an opening when Jackson stumbled back from a blow, but Diego had apparently seen or anticipated her shot. Before she could take aim, he grabbed a barstool and slung it at her.

She ducked and took the hard blow against her shoulder and side. Pain exploded through her arm and ribcage as the impact sent her sprawling to the ground. The tranquilizer gun slipped out of her sweating palm.

Whimpering, Daniela crawled forward, even knowing the futility of trying to reach Armando's gun. She wouldn't retrieve the weapon in time to pick it up, aim, and fire before Diego finished Jackson.

She felt her foolish arrogance, the poison of it right down to her bone marrow. She'd thought she could take on her uncle's cartel. But she had failed. For a moment, she felt like that insecure eighteen-year-old girl at her father's party all over again. Not good enough for anyone or anything.

She needed to end this. She needed to keep her son safe and save Jackson.

Stretching for the weapon, she grasped the gun, fingers tightening just as a shot rang out. Turning, she blinked several times, trying to process the scene before her. Jackson was on his hands and knees, panting for breath. Blood dripped from the corner of his mouth and from where his prior head injury looked to be rebleeding. Diego was down in a heap on the floor, and Sebastian stood over the Horseman, his own gun in his hand.

With a puzzled brow, Jackson stood unsteadily as blood pooled around Diego. Sebastian stared at the body with an expression of stunned shock. When Jackson reached slowly and grasped Sebastian's gun, her cousin didn't resist.

"Sebastian?" she ventured.

He turned a pair of weary eyes on her. "We always got along, you and I, Daniela. The family never treated either of us right. We were co-conspirators once—kids who found solace together in a cruel world. I couldn't get away with any sort of betrayal, constantly surrounded by *Padre's* loyal supporters. I brought the clumsy Jorge that night to your house and made him trip to tip you off. When my father ordered us to hunt you down, the only opportunity I saw to help you was to turn it into a game—put a cap on the number of people who could come after you. I'm sorry it was a flimsy plan."

He shuttered out a long sigh, took a pack of cigarettes out, then slid them back into his pocket. "I knew *El Chupacabra* was no threat. And I suspected Armando would help me against Emile. Diego was the wild card. I didn't know how to eliminate him. At least not without turning the cartel against me in the process." He wiped at his moistening eyes with the back of his left hand. "I'm tired of the fighting, Daniela. Tired of taking orders. You think me a coward?"

Daniela took the hand Jackson offered to help her stand. Her poor cousin had been called a coward all his life. As a mother, she never understood why some parents degraded their children, thinking harsh words were a means of motivation. They thought calling their child a coward would motivate them to try harder not to be. Calling them stupid would cause an effort to increase aptitude. Calling them weak would push them to be stronger. Perhaps there were some resilient children out there who responded in such a way, but disparaging words damaged the young psyche, resulting in self-doubt and low self-esteem. She knew this from experience.

"I think you've had a hard life," she told her cousin.

He glanced down at Armando, who slept on the floor.

"You're going to run away with him," Daniela said, hope in her voice.

Jackson, who'd been standing quietly with his gun pointed at the floor, placed his left hand on her shoulder—ever the silent supporter in her life.

Sebastian nodded. "He wanted me to. I thought it was impossible." His jaw tightened and his eyes narrowed as he glared over at Diego's dead body.

No, this was no coward, she knew.

"I thought there was no escape for me as long as Hermes was alive. And now he's not." He reached into his pocket and took out a small device Daniela recognized as the encrypted alert system her father had used to send signals. One password, one button, and thousands of his followers would be alerted who was the target for assassination.

Daniela gasped. "You've had this all this time, and you didn't you use it against me."

"I never wanted you dead, but I was too afraid to outright defy my father. The Four Horsemen seemed a better way to give you a fighting chance."

She shook her head and walked to him, wrapping him in a hug. "Running a cartel must have been a miserable life for someone like you who actually gives a damn." She eased back to look into his lovely brown eyes, keeping her hands on his shoulders.

"You could run it," Sebastian suggested with a wry smile as he raised the device to her.

She took it and a step back, happy to take something so utterly evil in order to see it destroyed. "No. I don't have a stomach for crime. When you have a son, you envision drug dealers manipulating children into using. I can't be a part of that."

"You're free now. Four horsemen are dead. Mostly."

She glanced at Armando.

"He's no threat to you," Sebastian said. "After today, we are dead men. We're going to bomb this saloon in hopes we'll be presumed dead. I'll ask that you keep our secret." He turned his gaze to Jackson.

"Anything Rider can do to spread word of our death would be much appreciated."

Jackson nodded his agreement.

Daniela stepped forward and wrapped her arms around Sebastian again. "I wish you freedom and happiness. If at all possible, visit me, if and when you think it's safe."

26

Jackson hung back as Daniela embraced Justin in a fierce hug. They stood in Mica's house, having just arrived back from Texas. Jackson's body and face still throbbed from the beating Diego had delivered, but he was too elated at Daniela having her freedom to be bothered by the pain.

"It's over, sweetheart. No more bad guys," Daniela told their son.

"Can we go home?"

"We can go anywhere we want to go." She drew back and ran a hand through his hair as a tear slid down her cheek.

Jackson wanted to wrap them both in a hug, but Justin's question had him hesitating. What if Daniela wanted to go back to her home and Justin's school? No problem. He could work anywhere for Rider. A different state was doable.

Justin glanced up at Jackson, and he could almost imagine the kid looked at him with some type of longing.

"Before we decide where we stay, I have something very important to tell you." Daniela stood and wiped a tear away. "Because of the wicked men—uh, enemy goons—after us, your dad and I couldn't be together. They kept us apart. Now we can be together. Justin, honey, Jackson is your father. I'm sorry I couldn't tell you sooner."

Justin stared at him, mouth agape.

Jackson shuffled his feet, tears pricking his eyes. "I'm sorry I couldn't be there for your first eight birthdays. I promise to be at all the rest."

Justin's tentative smile widened. He rushed to Jackson, who knelt to embrace him.

"I knew it." His son buried his face in Jackson's neck. "I wanted it to be you. I knew it."

Tears spilled from Jackson's eyes.

Nothing in life would top the way his heart swelled with his son in his arms. After shedding a tear for every year he'd missed, he blinked them away. He silently vowed to be the best father he could be. He honestly didn't know what that entailed, but he was coming from a place of love. Maybe there was a manual for this new role. If the FBI had taught him at least one thing, it was how to follow a manual.

"Can we move here, Mom? Can we live with Mr. Hart?" He glanced tentatively at Jackson. "With my dad?"

Dad... Jackson would never tire of Justin calling him that.

Daniela reached out and took Jackson's hand. "Yes, honey. We can stay with him."

Jackson thought his heart might burst from his chest and swallowed back another round of tears.

"What do you say we commemorate this moment with a meal out? What are you in the mood for?" Jackson asked.

"Steak," Justin said.

Daniela laughed.

Jackson stood, taking her hand in his while he kept his other hand on Justin's shoulder. "I know a great steak place."

FIVE DAYS LATER...

Daniela watched Jackson and Justin throw the football. A few minutes ago, they had been dueling with lightsabers as waves lapped at their feet with a backdrop of sunny skies and an ocean breeze.

She made a mental note to reapply sunscreen in thirty minutes... to both of them. Jackson was paler than his son.

The beach. A first, she marveled. Justin would have many firsts with his father now that they were free from WITSEC, from the cartel, and from fear.

She had been working out the logistics of moving her and Justin's things from their townhome out west to Atlanta, when Mica had offered Daniela a job after the debriefing. Rider SI needed someone to manage the finances and payroll. Daniela had been flabbergasted at how much trust Mica was willing to put in her. After taking a day to think about it, she had given her answer.

Yes, she would work for Rider SI. This was a wonderful way to give back to the team who'd helped give her and her family freedom from the cartel.

When their vacation was over, Daniela would start work. At the same time, she would need to enroll Justin in a new school... new family, new location, new life. This was the last time they would press the restart button.

She opened the novel she was reading and reread the note she was using as a bookmark. A few days after the Texas showdown, she had received a package in the mail from a post office box from a Robert Frost. She knew instantly it was from Sebastian and had been surprised to realize she'd forgotten he'd been a fan of poetry. The box contained her favorite red heels from the house she'd abandoned.

> Dearest Daniela,
>
> May you discover a world full of happiness and joy. I know I am.
>
> Con amor,
>
> Sebastian
>
> "I shall be telling this with a sigh

Somewhere ages and ages hence:
Two roads diverged in a wood, and I—
I took the one less traveled by,
And that has made all the difference."
—Robert Frost (The Road Not Taken)

Yes, she was discovering a world of happiness and joy made possible because Sebastian had taken a secret stand to help her against the cartel. She and her family were safe because of him and because of Rider SI.

She tucked the letter back into her book and focused on her two boys again. They had abandoned the ball and were up to Jackson's knees in the water. He scooped up Justin and tossed him into an oncoming wave. The boy shrieked, submerged, and came up laughing. As soon as he had his footing, he came at Jackson in playful wrestling. Effortlessly, Jackson picked him up and tossed him once more.

When they came back to where she sat under the sun umbrella, dripping wet, Jackson asked, "Everything okay?"

Justin sat out of earshot and started digging a hole in the sand.

Daniela sprang to her feet and wrapped her arms around him, not caring that the cold water soaked her dry suit. "Everything is *maravillos!*"

He picked her up, swinging her in a circle. "It is marvelous. And I want to marry you."

Her mouth parted in surprise.

"I'm sorry. Too fast." He set her on her feet, but didn't let go. "I've been thinking about it, even looking at rings on the internet, but I didn't intend to blurt that out."

She smiled at his reddening cheeks. The man who could face down a minotaur in a showdown was nervous about over-expressing his love for her. Her toes curled in the sand in excitement.

"I think Daniela Hart is a lovely name."

Eyes lighting with delight, he kissed her.

After savoring the kiss, she leaned back and pointed a playful finger at his bare chest. "But I still want a proper proposal over a nice dinner."

"You shall have it."

"And I want flowers, beautiful bright roses."

"Every day," he promised.

"Not every day. Only when you're feeling smitten."

"Yeah, so, every day."

She smiled and pressed her lips to his for another kiss.

He glanced back at Justin playing in the sand. "I'm sorry I had to miss some of his growing years. Especially early holidays when they're so magical for kids."

She shrugged in his arms. "So, we'll make fresh memories. And we can have more children, so we can share all of that."

His face lit in a smile. "Yeah? How many can I have?"

She chuckled. "How about you survive the diaper changing and toddler years and then decide how many you really want?"

"We'd better get started soon, then." He grinned and kissed her again.

MICA HUNG up the phone and sipped her chai latte in the quiet coffee shop as she waited for her meeting with Nash Rucker.

"That looked like an unpleasant conversation." Nash approached and took a seat.

He wore jeans and the same leather jacket from the first time they'd met. She suspected his motorcycle was parked somewhere outside.

"Special Agent Eddie Finch of the FBI is upset that he was called upon by the US Marshals as a character reference for me. The Marshals are wrapping up their paperwork as it relates to Daniela, who let them know she was officially out of WITSEC and would like to remain presumed dead in the abandoned town bombing a few days ago."

"Are they giving you grief?" Nash asked.

"No more than usual." Mica shrugged.

Daniela Rivera's case was miraculously closed. Sebastian and Armando had partially bombed the abandoned town as promised. Publicly, authorities were spinning the bombing to say Daniela César and Diego Aguilar had died, though human remains were difficult to identify. Privately, they only had one set of bones... Diego's.

Claire was leaking fake news on the internet, claiming the dead were Sebastian César, Diego Aguilar, and a woman. The hope was that the cartel would assume the woman was Daniela César, daughter of the late Alejandro César. Of the Four Horsemen, only Armando still lived, but he and Sebastian had fled—hopefully to somewhere peaceful, in the words of Daniela.

"How is your niece?" Mica asked.

"Recovering. They didn't hurt her, and they gave her oral sedatives. Consequently, she doesn't remember much. I'm in your debt for using your resources and helping me get her safely out of there. After the way I behaved, you didn't have to help me."

Nash had apologized several times now, and remorse was a strong character trait in Mica's book.

"Have you considered my offer?" Mica asked.

Nash rubbed his neck. "It's a generous offer. It's also surprising, considering we didn't have a great initial encounter."

She smirked. "I'm thinking first impressions aren't your strong suit."

He snorted. "Yeah, you got that right."

"You were under duress—suspended with a partner in the hospital."

"I still barged in and assaulted you."

"You've got a temper that could use pruning," she agreed. But she'd also heard from her team that Nash had performed with precision under pressure in Texas. He'd taken care to protect his DEA pals in addition to the Rider team. She was willing to help him get past his anger issues if it meant she earned another loyal and talented employee.

"If you hire me, you need to know my past isn't without demons."

"Then you won't be any different from most of my employees." She couldn't think of a single person she employed who didn't have skeletons in the proverbial closet.

"Yes, but some of mine haven't been laid to rest."

*****~~~~*****

FIND out what danger snares Nash and his brother Garret in *Rucker File*, the next action-packed Rider File.

THE RIDER FILES SERIES

Meridian File / Masters File / Box Set 1

McMillan File / Maltisse File /Box Set 2

Storm File / Sullivan File / Box Set 3

Sharp File / Sizani File / Box Set 4

2024: Rivera File / Rucker File / Box Set 5

2025: Richmond File / Redwood File / Box Set 6

DEAR READER

Want to keep in touch?

If you enjoyed this book and want to know about future releases by CB Samet you can CLICK HERE to sign up for my mailing list! I promise I won't spam you. I only send an email when I have a new book released, giveaways, or special discounts. You can also unsubscribe at any time.

If you loved this book, kindly let others know by posing a brief comment on social media or leave a review where you purchased it so readers can find their next favorite romantic suspense series.

Even more ways to follow me below!

Thank you for reading,
CB Samet

OTHER BOOKS BY CB SAMET

Looking for more romantic suspense? How about with an urban fantasy twist? Check out The Shadow Guardians trilogy.

Get *Raven's Flight, a prequel novella* for FREE. In my newsletter, you'll learn about me, special discounts, and new releases.

Raven's Flight, prequel novella

Raine Down, Book 1

Rosalyn's Run, novella

Storm Surge, Book 2

Anka's Orb, novella

Sky Fall, Book 3

The Dr. Whyte Adventure Novels

Thriller Series

Black Gold

Whyte Knight

Gray Horizon

Sweet Romantic Suspense

"Well-written... tales of love and ghosts."

— KIRKUS REVIEW

IN BOXED SETS

Romancing the Spirit Series #1

Sadie's Spirit / Willow's Windfall

Cassie's Chase / Phoebe's Pharaoh

Vanessa's Valentine / Autumn's Angel

Romancing the Spirit Series #2

Carol's Christmas / Allison's Alibi

Gracelynn's Genie / Michelle's Miracle

Heather's Hero / Chloe's Cupid

Romancing the Spirit Series #3

Sabrina's Storm / Jenny's Justice

Stella's Star / Gigi's Gift

Phoenix's Phantom / Fiona's Freedom

Love action/adventure and strong female leads in a fantasy world? Check out my other genre:

The Avant Champion Fantasy Series

The Avant Champion: Rising

Malakai: An Avant Champion Origin of Malos Story (prequel)

The Avant Champion: Honor

The Avant Champion: Ashes

Brothers' Bond: An Avant Champion Malakai Story

The Avant Champion: Conquest

Isabel: An Avant Champion novelette

The Avant Champion: Redeem